The Mystery at Magnolia Mansion

"I wish we had our bags," Nancy said as she and Bess settled in their room at Magnolia Mansion. "I want to start reading Amelia's books tonight."

"You're unbelievable," Bess said. "Don't you ever get tired?" She stifled a yawn. "I'm going to wash up and then drop into bed."

Bess started toward the door, and Nancy leaned her head back on the chair. Suddenly, a muffled scream made her jerk upright.

There, in the open doorway, stood a ghostly figure in a long, white gown. And one of its hands was clapped tightly over Bess's mouth!

Nancy Drew
Mystery Stories

Available from MINSTREL Books

NANCY DREW MYSTERY STORIES®

97

NANCY DREW®

THE MYSTERY AT MAGNOLIA MANSION

CAROLYN KEENE

A MINSTREL® BOOK

PUBLISHED BY POCKET BOOKS

New York   London   Toronto   Sydney   Tokyo   Singapore

A MINSTREL PAPERBACK *ORIGINAL*

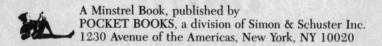

A Minstrel Book, published by
POCKET BOOKS, a division of Simon & Schuster Inc.
1230 Avenue of the Americas, New York, NY 10020

ISBN: 0-671-69282-8

First Minstrel Books printing October 1990

10 9 8 7 6 5 4 3 2

Contents

THE MYSTERY AT
MAGNOLIA MANSION

1

Ticket to Mystery

Bess Marvin slumped back into the lounge chair with a dreamy expression. "What an ending." She sighed as she closed the book she'd been reading.

Nancy Drew slid her sunglasses down her nose and looked at Bess over the lenses. The two girls were sunbathing near the pool at the River Heights Country Club. "How many times have you read that book?" Nancy asked, smiling at her friend.

"Four," Bess replied seriously, "and it gets better each time. Rhett Reynolds, the hero, is just so cool—and totally gorgeous. I cry every time he saves Angel from her rotten cousin."

"I've noticed," Nancy said, her blue eyes twinkling. She took the book from Bess and looked at the title. "*Southern Flame*. Sounds *real* historical."

"It is!" said Bess, tossing her long blond hair over her shoulders. "The author, Amelia Beaufort, spends months researching her facts. This story takes place in South Carolina during the Civil War. Besides, Amelia Beaufort's books are a lot more interesting than *that*." Bess pointed to the issue of *Crime Today*, which lay facedown on Nancy's lap.

"I don't know about that," Nancy said, settling back in her chair. "There's an article on private investigators in here. And one on breaking codes. I think that's pretty interesting stuff."

"You would," Bess teased. "But I suppose reading that magazine is the price you have to pay for being River Heights' best-known amateur detective."

Nancy sat up and swung her long, slender legs over the side of the lounge. She flipped rapidly through the pages of the magazine, stopping when she found what she was looking for. "Tell me this isn't interesting," she challenged Bess. "Here's an article on famous people who have disappeared without a trace."

"Really?" Bess sipped her soda. "Does it mention Amelia Beaufort in there?"

A puzzled expression came over Nancy's face. "Amelia Beaufort is missing?"

Bess picked up the copy of *Southern Flame* and tapped the photo on the back cover. A striking brunette smiled from a posed publicity shot. "I've been writing to Amelia Beaufort for about a year and a half, ever since I took that English course. You remember, the one where we had to contact a favorite author."

"That's right," Nancy recalled. "And you chose Amelia Beaufort?"

Bess nodded. "I wrote and told her how much I loved her books. She wrote back a really nice letter, and we've been writing ever since. At least until . . ."

"Until when?" Nancy asked.

"Until about three months ago," said Bess. "I haven't heard a word from her. She used to write once a month."

Nancy rolled her eyes. "Bess, that doesn't exactly make her a missing person."

"I know," said Bess, "but something else seems strange to me. Amelia publishes a new book every summer. It's July already—and no book. That's why I'm rereading *Southern Flame.*"

Nancy pulled her long, reddish blond hair away from her forehead and began applying sunblock to her face. "Maybe Amelia's behind schedule on her new book and she's too busy to write you."

Bess looked doubtful. "I just have this feeling that something is wrong. Amelia wrote to me last year, even though her book *Rebel Love* was a week overdue. It's not like her."

"Maybe she's got writer's block," Nancy suggested.

"Forget it," said Bess, getting to her feet. "You're

not taking me seriously." A mischievous look came into her light blue eyes. "I'm sorry I ever wrote and told Amelia you were the best detective in the world. I even told her you'd make a great subject for a book."

"Flattery will get you everywhere, Bess," Nancy joked. She stood up and adjusted her bright blue one-piece swimsuit. "Let's take a swim." Before Bess could respond, Nancy grabbed her friend by the wrist and jumped into the pool, pulling Bess in with her.

Seconds later, both girls surfaced.

"You rat!" sputtered Bess.

"Come on," Nancy replied. "I'll race you to the other side."

"Okay," Bess said with a grin. "It might help me to work off some calories."

A few hours later, Nancy steered her blue sports car toward Bess's house. The warm summer breeze whipped the girls' hair around their faces.

"Stop at our mailbox, okay?" Bess requested as they reached the box at the end of the Marvins' driveway. "I want to see if this month's issue of *Fashion Focus* came today."

Nancy braked, and Bess leaned out the car window to open the mailbox. "No magazine," Bess said glumly. "Might as well bring in the rest of the mail."

Bess drew her head back in the car and began

flipping through the stack of letters she'd taken from the box.

"This is strange," she said, holding up a long white envelope. "A travel agent sent me a letter."

"Did you write away for information or something?" asked Nancy, pulling the car up the drive.

"Nope," said Bess, frowning as she opened the envelope. "It's probably junk mail."

Nancy looked into the envelope. "It's not junk mail," she said. "It looks as if there are two airline tickets in there."

Bess took out the tickets. "They're to Charleston, South Carolina."

"That's great," said Nancy. "Are they from a relative?"

Bess shook her head. "This is totally strange," she murmured. "One of these tickets has *your* name on it."

"What! Let me see that." Nancy snatched the ticket from Bess. "You're right!" she exclaimed. "And they're dated for two days from now."

Nancy and Bess exchanged puzzled glances.

"I don't get it," said Bess. "Maybe Mom knows something about this."

The girls headed up the walkway to Bess's house. "Mom!" Bess called as they entered the cool front hall.

"I'm upstairs," came her mother's voice in response.

"I'll go ask her if she knows what this is about,"

5

said Bess. She was halfway up the stairs when the phone on the hallway table rang. "Would you get that, Nancy?"

"Hi, this is the Marvin household," Nancy said cheerfully into the receiver.

"Bess, Bess Marvin?" a woman's voice on the other end whispered in a thick southern drawl.

"No, she's—" Nancy began.

The woman didn't seem to hear Nancy. "This is Amelia Beaufort. Bess, I need your help. You and your friend, Miss Drew. You must come quickly."

"This is Nancy Drew," Nancy cut in. "I'll get Bess. She'll be so excited to—"

"Miss Drew, please say you'll come." The woman cut Nancy off once again. "There's no one else I can turn to. My beloved Magnolia Mansion—it's turning against me." Nancy heard static crackling over the line as the woman continued. "There's danger lurking everywhere. Terrible danger."

"What kind of danger?" asked Nancy.

But no one answered.

The line had gone dead.

2

Southern Hospitality

Bess came back down the stairs. "My mom has no idea who would send us airline tickets to South Carolina," she said. "It's a real mystery." Bess paused when she saw Nancy's face. "What's up, Nan?"

"I know who sent the tickets," Nancy replied slowly. "That was Amelia Beaufort on the phone, and she wants us to come to South Carolina." She quickly filled Bess in on the conversation she'd had with Amelia.

"That's so strange," said Bess, looking concerned. "I had a feeling that Amelia was in some kind of trouble."

Nancy sat down on the bottom step. "She

sounded more than terrified," she said. "She sounded . . . frantic."

"Magnolia Mansion is Amelia's home," mused Bess. "How could a house turn against you?"

"Beats me," said Nancy. "Do you know anything about Amelia? What are her letters like?"

Bess shrugged. "She talks about her books mostly. She never says much about her private life at all."

A faint smile formed on Nancy's lips. "And I thought it was going to be a dull summer." She got to her feet. "I have to go home and make sure it's okay with Dad that I'm taking this trip."

"So we're going to Magnolia Mansion," said Bess, grinning at her friend. "You never can resist a good mystery." A worried look passed over Bess's face. "I'm not so sure I'm as excited about going down there. 'Danger lurking everywhere' sounds eerie. How about going without me?"

"Oh, no," said Nancy, laughing. "You got me into this, Bess Marvin, and you're coming with me." She placed her hands on Bess's shoulders and turned her toward the stairs. "So get upstairs and start packing. Magnolia Mansion, here we come."

"We hope you enjoyed your flight," the flight attendant said over the address system. "Have a pleasant stay in Charleston."

Nancy and Bess stood in the aisle of the jet,

8

waiting to disembark. "I hope Amelia is here to pick us up," Bess said nervously as the line of passengers inched forward.

"Me, too," said Nancy. They hadn't been able to tell the author that they were coming. They had called Charleston information for her phone number, only to discover that it was unlisted. Besides, Nancy had a hunch that the other day, when her phone conversation with Amelia abruptly ended, the phone line at Magnolia Mansion had been cut.

Inside the airport terminal, a small group of people hovered at the gate to meet the flight. Nancy scanned the faces, looking for Amelia Beaufort. No one resembling the author appeared.

"Well," Bess said with a sigh, "looks like we're on our own." She picked up her overstuffed carry-on bag and swung her bulky purse over her shoulder.

Nancy laughed at her weighed-down friend. "What did you pack in there, anyway?"

"For your information, this bag contains all twenty-two Amelia Beaufort novels," huffed Bess. "Remember, you asked me to bring all of her books."

"I wanted to read them to learn more about Amelia," Nancy said. "I didn't know there were twenty-two of them!" She grabbed one of the handles on Bess's bag and helped her carry it over to the baggage claim area.

They set the bag down near a conveyor belt where the larger suitcases were arriving from the plane. Nancy and Bess watched for their luggage as the bags circled slowly on the belt.

"My father says Charleston's a beautiful, historic old city," Nancy said to Bess. "Even if we never meet the mysterious Ms. Beaufort, we should have a great time."

"Excuse me, ladies," came a silky, southern-accented voice. "Your names wouldn't be Bess and Nancy, would they?"

Nancy and Bess turned. Standing behind them was a handsome young man in his early twenties. His hair was dark and wavy, and his eyes were ice blue. "I'm Rex Beaufort. My aunt Amelia sent me to come get you all."

Nancy held out her hand. "I'm Nancy Drew," she said. "And this is Bess Marvin."

Bess smiled. "How did you know who we were?"

Rex shook their hands. "My aunt told me to look for two young ladies. I didn't see any others," he explained simply.

"There go our suitcases," cried Bess, pointing.

Rex pulled them off the conveyor belt. "I'm parked outside," he said, carrying the two cases toward the door.

"He's adorable," Bess whispered as they hurried along behind him.

"Think so?" asked Nancy. "There's something about him I don't like."

"What's not to like?" asked Bess, her eyes twinkling. "He's a hunk."

Nancy smiled at her friend but didn't say anything more as the two girls followed Rex to the parking lot. The hot, humid night air seemed to envelop them like a damp blanket. Rex led them to an old pickup truck and threw their suitcases and the heavy carry-on into the back. "I'm sorry this old heap isn't suitable for the president and vice president of the Amelia Beaufort fan club," he said.

Nancy and Bess exchanged glances. Why hadn't Amelia told Rex who they really were? Nancy wondered. Amelia must not trust her nephew.

"Being officers of such a big club must keep you two very busy," he said, smirking as he helped them up into the cab of the truck.

Nancy frowned. I don't trust him, either, she thought. His tone seemed almost mocking.

"We don't mind the work," said Bess. "We adore your aunt."

Rex muttered something under his breath as he started the engine. He steered out of the airport parking lot and onto the highway. They traveled in silence for about fifteen minutes.

Nancy sat next to the window, letting the hot, sticky air blow her hair. They soon turned off the highway onto a dark, tree-lined road.

Nancy glanced over at Rex. His mouth was set in a tight line. She wondered what was going through his mind. "Do you live with your aunt?" she asked.

"Just for the summer," he said. "I grew up in South Carolina, but now I go to college in Boston. Aunt Amelia asked me to spend the summer to help with the old place. I needed a summer job so here I am."

"We tried to call and say we were coming," Bess said, "but the number is unlisted. We were hoping Ms. Beaufort would call us again, but she didn't. We didn't know if anyone was going to come to meet us."

"That's me, Magnolia Mansion's official greeter," Rex replied sarcastically. "Aunt Amelia didn't call you back because the phones at the mansion have been down for the last two days."

"What's the problem?" asked Nancy.

"Don't know," said Rex. "The phone company was at the house today to take a look."

Just then the truck motor coughed, sputtered, and died.

Rex pounded the steering wheel. "Great!" he yelled. "I should have known this old wreck wouldn't make it. Nothing works around this dump!" With a quick glance at Nancy and Bess, he recovered his smooth coolness. "Well, ladies, this is as far as I go. But you're in luck. The driveway is just down the road."

He opened the door and jumped out. "I'd escort you, but I'm going to try to get this fabulous vehicle moving again."

Bess and Nancy peered through the windshield

12

into the dark night. A few paces to their right, a stone column, overgrown with vines, was the only sign of an entrance.

Bess clutched her purse to her chest. "Uh, maybe we should wait for you."

"It's after ten," said Rex, checking his watch. "This might take a while. I'll leave your suitcases in the hallway outside your room when I come up."

"That sounds great," said Nancy as she climbed out of the truck. Rex immediately opened the hood and began tinkering with the engine.

"See you in the morning," Nancy called. She took Bess by the arm and steered her friend up the road.

"This is not my idea of fun," Bess whispered loudly. "This place gives me the creeps." The edge of the drive was overgrown with brush and vines. Nancy could see azaleas and boxwoods peeking out from beneath a smothering jungle of weeds. Above them, a canopy of trees hid the sky. Cascades of long, silvery moss flowed from their branches. It was obvious that Magnolia Mansion hadn't had a gardener's care for many years.

"Now I know how Hansel and Gretel felt." Bess shivered. "What is that horrible stuff all over the trees?"

"Spanish moss," Nancy replied. Suddenly she stopped walking. Silhouetted against the night sky, Magnolia Mansion rose before them like a fortress. The glow from an almost-full moon bathed its roof and sides in silvery light. A white, two-tiered porch with graceful columns jutted out from the front of the rectangular building. Crumbling stone steps rose up to an ornately carved door. The house had once been beautiful, but like the grounds, it was now badly in need of some repair.

"I feel like I've just walked onto the set of a horror film," Bess whispered.

"I know what you mean," Nancy agreed. Slowly they approached the old steps and climbed up to the wide door. "Here goes," said Nancy, grasping the heavy brass knocker.

After two loud raps, they waited. No one came to the door.

"Nobody's home. Maybe we should leave," said Bess hopefully.

"We can't chicken out now," said Nancy. She was about to knock again when the door opened with a loud creak. Staring out at them was a thin, sour-faced woman with dark hair set in tight curls around her face. Her small eyes darted back and forth as she scrutinized them.

"I'm Bess Marvin, and this is Nancy—" Bess began.

"I know," interrupted the woman. "Come in." She opened the door to a dimly lit hall. "Miss Amelia asked me to wait up for you. She has gone to bed. She needs her rest. Your room is upstairs, the first one on the right," she said curtly.

14

"Thanks," said Nancy, stepping into the long hall. Bess followed close at her heels. For a moment, the two stared in awe at the carved woodwork and high, arched ceiling. A crystal chandelier hung above them, its glass pendants twinkling in the dim light.

When they looked back to the woman, she was gone.

"Nancy!" cried Bess. "That woman disappeared."

"No, she didn't," Nancy said calmly. "Look."

Bess followed Nancy's gaze into an unlit dining room off the hallway. She was just in time to see the woman walk through a door and out of the room. Bess let her breath out in a whoosh. "She could have said good night," said Bess shakily.

"Come on," said Nancy. "Let's see what excitement lurks upstairs."

Portraits of grim-faced men and women stared out at them from the wall along the spiral staircase. When the girls reached the second floor, Nancy nodded toward the first door on the right. Slowly she turned the knob and pushed the door open. With a sigh of relief, the girls hurried into the spacious room.

Nancy threw her purse down on the large canopied bed, then flopped into a wing chair in front of a fireplace.

"A cool fan would feel great right now," Bess

said. She pulled back the heavy velvet curtains. A damp breeze wafted into the room from the open window.

"I wish we had our bags," Nancy said. "I want to start reading Amelia's books tonight."

"You're unbelievable," Bess said. "Don't you ever get tired?" She stifled a yawn. "I'm going to wash up and then drop into bed."

Bess started toward the door, and Nancy leaned her head back on the chair. Actually it *had* been a long day and she did feel a little tired. She closed her eyes. Suddenly, a muffled scream made her jerk them open again.

There, in the open doorway, stood a ghostly figure in a long, white gown. And one of its hands was clapped tightly over Bess's mouth!

3

Meeting Ms. Beaufort

"Bess!" Nancy sprang from the chair.

Bess twisted her body and broke loose from the ghostly figure. She stumbled back toward Nancy, and for a moment, the two just stared at the figure in the doorway.

Finally Nancy relaxed. The ghost was actually an older woman, whose long silvery hair and white nightgown had made her look like an apparition for a second.

"What's going on?" Nancy demanded.

"Shh!" The woman put a crooked finger to her lips and listened for a moment. Then, seeming satisfied that no one had heard, she smiled at the two girls.

"Welcome to Magnolia Mansion," the woman

whispered. The girls noticed for the first time that she was leaning on a cane.

"Ms. Beaufort?" said Bess in a surprised voice.

The woman nodded and held out her hand. Her fingers were gnarled and bent. "Please excuse my dramatic entrance," she said, shaking Bess's hand. "I wanted to speak to you without anyone hearing. I didn't expect you to be standing at the door. I only wanted to stop you from crying out."

"I *was* pretty startled," replied Bess. "I'm Bess and this is Nancy."

"I'm so happy you're here," said Amelia. "You can't imagine how glad I am."

Nancy was surprised at Amelia Beaufort's appearance and could tell Bess was, too. The picture on the back of the book had shown a woman in her forties with long brown hair. Yet, now that she had a closer look, Nancy could see the resemblance. The photo on the book must have been taken at least twenty years ago.

Amelia seemed to read Nancy's thoughts. "I suppose you were both expecting the young author pictured on my books." She laughed. "My agent insists on using that old shot. Not that I blame him. This old face wouldn't sell many books."

"That's not true," Bess protested, settling on the edge of the bed.

Nancy dropped down beside Bess, and Amelia settled into the armchair.

"Your phone call sounded pretty urgent," Nancy

said, eager to have some of her questions about this mystery answered. "What can we help you with?"

"I'm sorry I never called back. The phones have been out," said Amelia. "Today, when we finally got someone in for repairs, the phone man told me the line had been cut."

Nancy raised her eyebrows. "I've been wondering if that's why we were cut off."

Amelia nodded. "That's why I need you, Nancy. For the last few months, strange things like that have been happening. I don't know who—or what —is causing them."

"What else has happened?" asked Nancy.

"Last week I had a car accident," Amelia continued in a hushed tone. "I stepped on the brake, but the car didn't stop. I hit the pillar at the entrance. The front end of my car was totally ruined."

"Are you okay?" asked Bess.

Amelia nodded toward her cane. "I'm using this because I pulled a tendon. Other than that, and frayed nerves, I'm fine, thank heavens." Amelia stood and walked over to an old dresser. Her steps were slow and careful, as if each one was painful. Bending down, she pulled open a drawer and took out a copy of *Southern Flame*, the book Bess had just finished rereading.

"Before that, I found this," said Amelia, opening the book. The middle pages had been slashed. Written across them in a childish scrawl was the word *Traitor*.

" 'Traitor,' " said Bess. "Why would someone ruin your book and call you a traitor?"

"I don't know." Amelia shook her head sadly. "I didn't know where to turn. Then I remembered your telling me what a wonderful detective Nancy is."

"She's the best," said Bess loyally.

Nancy smiled at Bess. "I'll certainly try my best to help you figure out who's behind this, Ms. Beaufort," she said.

"Please, both of you, call me Amelia," said the woman. "Let's go downstairs and have a snack. But if anyone comes along, pretend to be the president and vice president of my fan club."

"We've already done that with your nephew," Nancy replied. "Why is that necessary?"

Amelia laughed nervously. "It's not that I don't trust Rex. I simply don't want to worry him."

"Are you sure?" Nancy asked skeptically.

"Oh, yes, perfectly sure," insisted Amelia. "You may think I'm crazy for what I'm about to say—but I wonder if the culprit is a spirit from the past."

Bess gulped. "You mean a ghost?"

"This house is rich in history," Amelia explained. "Perhaps a spirit is restless. Maybe my writings have displeased one of them." Amelia covered her face with her hands.

Bess jumped to her feet and put her arms around the woman. In a minute, Amelia seemed to recover her composure.

20

"Maybe we should explore some other possibilities first," Nancy said tactfully.

"You're probably right," said Amelia. "These past few months have rattled my nerves. I'm not myself at all. Come, let's have that snack I promised."

Nancy and Bess followed Amelia out of the room and down the stairs. About halfway down, Amelia pointed to the portrait of a man in a gray Confederate uniform. "My great-grandfather," she said in a whisper, as though the portrait could hear. "Here in Charleston, he's a Civil War hero." Nancy noticed a slight catch in Amelia's voice.

"On the plane, I read that most of this area was burned during the war," Nancy said.

"It was," said Amelia. She pointed to a painting of a woman with thick dark hair caught in a bun at the back of her neck. "Magnolia Mansion was spared only because my great-grandmother turned it into a hospital for children with smallpox. The Yankees didn't go near it for fear of catching the disease."

"So, both your great-grandparents were heroes," Nancy pointed out.

"I suppose they were," agreed Amelia. "I never really thought of it that way."

On the ground floor, they passed through the dark dining room into the kitchen. When Amelia switched on the light, Nancy saw that the floor and counters were spotless.

"This is Louise Brewton's domain," Amelia told them. "She's my housekeeper. I trust she was here to let you in."

"She didn't seem pleased to see us," said Bess.

"Louise doesn't like to stay up past nine-thirty," said Amelia. "I hated to ask her to wait, but I just couldn't keep my eyes open. If I hadn't heard you come up the stairs, I might be asleep still."

Just then, the kitchen door swung open with a bang. Rex stood in the doorway. "Aunt Amelia, what are you doing up?" he asked in an accusing voice.

"Greeting my guests, of course," Amelia replied stiffly.

"Remember what we talked about," he said, a warning note in his voice.

"You needn't worry, Rex," Amelia replied.

Rex's eyes narrowed as he took in Bess and Nancy. "Your bags are upstairs in the hall," he told them. Then, with one last frown at his aunt, he disappeared the way he came in.

"What was that about?" Nancy asked after a moment.

"Oh, you'll have to excuse Rex," said Amelia. "He doesn't take to the members of my fan club. He calls them silly twits. He thinks they just eat my food, tire me, and distract me from my writing."

"That's why he's so rude?" asked Bess.

"I believe so. He's just being protective of me," Amelia answered.

22

I wonder, thought Nancy doubtfully. Is that what's really behind his behavior? Or is there another reason why he's annoyed that we're here?

Amelia poured them each a glass of lemonade. She took a plate of homemade pecan cookies from the sideboard. "Louise is a marvelous cook," she said as she bit into a cookie. "Try one."

Nancy took a cookie, still lost in her thoughts about Rex. There was a question she had to ask Amelia. She hesitated, not sure how to word it. "Amelia, who inherits Magnolia Mansion from you?"

"Rex, of course," Amelia answered.

Why doesn't that surprise me? thought Nancy, leaning back in her chair. Right now, Rex was her number-one suspect. "Who else lives here?" she asked.

"It's just me, Rex, Louise, and her husband, Miles," said Amelia. "Actually Louise and Miles live above the garage on the grounds."

"Anyone else?" Nancy pressed.

"Oh, and Roslyn Sillay. She's my secretary," Amelia added. "I hired her about three months ago when my hands got too sore to write. Arthritis, you know. My agent recommended her."

Nancy and Bess exchanged glances. Three months ago was when Amelia had stopped writing to Bess.

"Amelia," Bess said gently, "I've been wondering why you stopped writing to me."

The author's brow creased into a puzzled expression. "I wrote you just last week. I told you I was sending the tickets."

"I haven't received a letter from you in three months," Bess told her.

"That's impossible!" cried Amelia. "I write you on the fifth of every month. I give Roslyn the letters to address and mail."

Nancy raised her eyebrows.

"Don't go accusing that dear girl," Amelia said, noticing Nancy's expression. "The fault may lie with the post office. I'll get to the bottom of this in the morning."

Bess finished her lemonade. "I'm glad you didn't stop writing," she said happily. "I thought you'd forgotten about me."

"Absolutely not," said Amelia, patting Bess's hand. "You write lovely, expressive letters."

A radiant smile crossed Bess's face. "Thank you," she said.

Amelia smiled back. "Now I must be getting back to bed," she said, pulling herself up from her chair. "I am suddenly so fatigued."

"Bess, I'll do the dishes, and you can help Amelia up the stairs," Nancy suggested.

"Okay," Bess agreed, taking the woman's arm.

The three said good night as Bess escorted Amelia from the kitchen. Nancy washed and dried the glasses. The house seemed ominously quiet—

as if it were silently watching her every move. Goosebumps tingled up Nancy's arms.

Boy, you are really imagining things, Nancy told herself. She laid the dishcloth on the counter, snapped off the light, and headed out of the kitchen.

Upstairs, the hallway was completely dark. The moon must be behind a cloud, Nancy thought as she felt along the hallway for the entrance to her room. She couldn't even see the door.

Suddenly something caught Nancy's eye. A small yellow light was flickering at the end of the long hall. Nancy peered into the darkness. Was the light coming toward her?

Nancy quietly inched down the hall toward the light. It was definitely coming closer to her. It looked like the flicker of a candle. "Hello?" she called out softly.

There was no answer. But the light stopped moving. "Who's there?" Nancy asked.

The "flame" quivered, then went out.

4

A Door Opens

Nancy drew her body up against the wall, her heart pounding. She listened for footsteps. There were none. "Who's there?" she said again, trying to sound braver than she felt.

A sixth sense told Nancy that whoever had been there was gone. But how could that be? She hadn't even heard footsteps. It was as if the person holding the light had been swallowed up by the silent house.

Then Nancy realized something. There was a smell in the air. It was the burning wax from the candle. Keeping close to the wall, she moved toward the scent.

The smell became stronger about three steps from where she'd been standing. As Nancy continued down the hall, the smell began to fade. She moved back to where the smell had been strongest.

This is about where the light went out, she decided. There's got to be some kind of doorway or passageway here.

Nancy moved her hands along the wall, feeling for a crack or hinge of some kind. After a few moments, she sighed. It was crazy trying to find anything in this pitch-blackness. It would have to wait for the morning.

Nancy reached into the pocket of her pants and pulled out a quarter. She quietly placed it on the floor where she was standing and hoped no one would pick it up before she returned. In the morning, the quarter would show her where the light had disappeared.

Following the wall, Nancy found her way back to her room. Bess was already asleep. She'd pulled their bags into the room and left them standing near the door.

Nancy knew she should be exhausted, too, but her mind was racing.

Was Rex trying to get his aunt out of the way so he could take over the mansion? That was a strong motive, yet he didn't seem all that fond of the place. And why hadn't Roslyn Sillay sent Bess's letters? One letter might get lost, but not three. Then there was the matter of the mysterious light in the hall.

Nancy unzipped Bess's bulky carry-on bag. "Let's see what these can tell me," she whispered to herself as she rummaged through the books in the bag. All the books were paperbacks, except for one. *Love in Atlanta*, Nancy read, lifting the book from the bag. A quick check told her that it had been published by a different publisher than the other books. It had been copyrighted almost thirty years ago. I bet this is her first book, Nancy thought. I might as well begin at the beginning.

Curling up in the wing chair near the fireplace, Nancy opened the book. Its pages were yellow with age. "Captain Lance Mulgrew tipped his soldier's cap to the breathtakingly beautiful Miss Amy Fairchild. His handsome blue eyes twinkled with rakish charm."

Nancy chuckled to herself. Oh, brother, how corny! She shook her head as she thought about Bess reading these books over and over again. But to her surprise she quickly found herself engrossed in the historical romance.

"Nancy, Nancy! Wake up!"

Slowly Nancy's eyes opened. She was still sitting in the wing chair. Bess was shaking her shoulder. *Love in Atlanta* lay half open on her lap. Rubbing her eyes, Nancy saw that it was morning.

"Couldn't put it down, could you?" said Bess brightly. "That's what happens with Amelia Beaufort books."

"It's not the kind of thing I usually like, but

28

reading it in this room made it seem very real,"
Nancy said.

"Go on, admit it, you've got the bug," Bess
teased. She picked up the book. "You found my
prize book, too. This book is out of print. I got it at a
tag sale in someone's garage. It's the very first book
Amelia Beaufort published. Did it reveal any
clues?"

Nancy crossed the room and unzipped her suitcase. "Sort of," she said, pulling out a denim skirt
and a cotton T-shirt. "The house in this book is
obviously modeled on Magnolia Mansion. And in
the book, the house has several secret passage-
ways."

Bess looked puzzled. "Do you think the passage-
ways have anything to do with what's been happening at the mansion?"

"Could be," replied Nancy. She quickly filled
her friend in on what had happened the night
before. "I'm sure of one thing," Nancy continued.
"Whoever was lurking in the hall last night disappeared through a secret door."

Bess dropped down onto the bed. "I don't know,
Nancy, maybe Amelia's right. Maybe there are
restless spirits lurking around this place."

Nancy laughed and quickly pulled on her
clothes. "Don't worry, Bess, it wasn't a ghost, and
whoever it was is long gone. Let's check out the
hallway, though, and see if we can find any clues."

She opened her suitcase and pulled out a small flashlight. "We'll need this if we find a secret passageway."

Bess still looked nervous, but she got up and put on a pink cotton sundress. She followed Nancy out the door.

In the hall, things were quiet. Nancy checked her watch. It was seven-thirty. "Hopefully, they're not early risers around here," she whispered to Bess.

It took only minutes for Nancy to find the quarter she'd dropped the night before. She studied the wall above it. Dark mahogany panels covered the bottom half of the wall. Each panel was about a foot wide, and separated from the others by beveled grooves. It was the perfect place to hide a doorway.

Nancy dropped to her knees and felt along the ornate molding near the floor. Suddenly her fingers felt a hairline crack running along the molding. "Here's the door," she whispered excitedly.

"You're kidding!" gasped Bess.

Nancy traced the crack. Sure enough, it rose up along one of the grooves. "But how does this thing open?" she wondered aloud.

"What if someone comes along?" asked Bess, sounding panicked.

"You keep watch," Nancy instructed. "We'll say I lost a contact lens or something if someone comes."

"Sure, and you just happen to be looking for it near a secret passageway," Bess responded.

"Keep your fingers crossed that no one comes," said Nancy, not looking up from the paneling.

Nancy frowned as she concentrated on finding a way into the passageway. "There's no lever or anything here," she muttered. She searched the top molding, which was level with her shoulders. The crack continued along just below the molding. There had to be a handle or some kind of hinge.

Then it came to her.

"Of course," she said, getting back down on her knees. "The door doesn't open, it lifts." She put her hands on the upper part of a smooth panel and pushed.

"It's moving!" cried Bess.

"Shh!" said Nancy. The door moved up silently and slid easily into a space in the wall above it. "This is the only thing in this house that doesn't creak," Nancy whispered. "Someone has oiled this recently."

Nancy stooped and stepped into the dark space. Inside, the ceiling was high enough for her to stand. A dark, narrow passageway stretched in front of her.

"Bess," whispered Nancy, "I'm going to close the door. I'll rap twice when I'm ready to come out. You rap back once if the coast is clear. Rap twice if it's not. Okay?"

"Be careful, Nancy," Bess said in a worried tone.

"I won't be long," Nancy assured her, sliding the

31

door down. Using her penlight, Nancy could see several feet in front of her. She walked slowly along the narrow corridor.

"Oooof!" Suddenly Nancy stumbled forward. She'd been so busy looking ahead, she hadn't noticed the opening below her feet. Narrow, rickety steps led downward. Probably to the first floor, Nancy guessed as she went down the steep stairs.

At the bottom of the stairs, the passageway veered off to the right. The air grew colder and colder. I'm going underground, Nancy realized.

After another five minutes, a glimmering of daylight broke through the darkness. Nancy looked up and saw a hatchway. Heavy boards had been nailed across it. There was no way Nancy could pry them loose by herself.

Now she was more confused than ever. Where had the person who ducked in here last night gone? There has to be another way out of here, she told herself.

She turned back, sweeping her flashlight along the walls in search of another hidden door.

Where are you? Nancy thought, frustrated. Just then her foot hit something hard lying on the floor. Aiming her flashlight down, she spotted an oval piece of metal. "Confederate Army," she read as she picked up the object. It's a belt buckle, she realized. The buckle felt heavy in her hands. I bet this is authentic, too, she thought.

She slipped the buckle into her skirt pocket and

made her way back up the narrow stairs to the second floor. She found the secret door and listened. It was quiet on the other side. She rapped once and waited.

There was no answering rap from Bess.

Nancy tried again. Still no reply.

"Bess!" she whispered loudly. Nothing.

A cold panic ran up Nancy's spine. What was going on out there? Was Bess all right?

Nancy pushed on the panel. It didn't move. She put her shoulder into it, pushing with all her strength. Still, the panel didn't budge.

At once, a horrible thought hit her.

She was stuck inside the secret passage, and there was no way out.

5

Writer's Block

"No, I didn't hear anything." Nancy suddenly heard Bess's voice through the panel.

"I distinctly heard a knock," came a male voice. Nancy recognized it immediately as Rex's.

"Oh," Bess said with a fluttery laugh, "that must have been me hitting the wall. I saw a mosquito and went to squish it."

"Well, go easy on the woodwork. This is an old house," said Rex, with the same snide tone that Nancy had noted last night. "Are you coming down to breakfast?"

"Um . . . in a minute," Nancy heard Bess stalling. "I . . . uh . . . lost my contact lens here. I have to find it."

Nancy hoped Rex would stay true to his rude

character and not offer to help Bess. "Don't take too long," he said. "Louise doesn't wait breakfast forever."

"Okay," Bess replied. Nancy let out a breath as she heard Rex's footsteps recede down the hallway.

A moment later, the door of the passageway slid up.

"I thought I was going to be trapped in there forever," said Nancy, stepping out into the hall.

"I didn't know what to do," said Bess. "Just as you knocked, I spotted Rex coming down the hall from his room. I was afraid to knock back and I was worried you'd just come bursting out. I leaned down as hard as I could against the panel. I hope I didn't scare you."

"Just until I heard your voice," Nancy admitted, sliding the door back down behind her.

"That was too close, Nancy. Did you find anything?"

"The passageway leads outside, but the opening at the other end is boarded up," Nancy told Bess. "There's got to be another way out. I couldn't find it, though." Nancy took the buckle from her pocket. "I did find this."

"How exciting!" said Bess. "Wait till Amelia sees it."

"Let's not tell Amelia everything just yet," Nancy said. "I want to see more of our hostess before I decide to trust her completely."

"You don't trust Amelia?" said Bess. "Why not?"

"How do we know she's telling us the truth?" asked Nancy. "You have to admit that—sweet as she seems—she is a bit odd."

"I suppose," Bess conceded. "But I'm sure she's just an innocent victim."

A noise behind them made the two girls turn.

"And isn't this Oriental rug in the hallway gorgeous?" Nancy quickly said to Bess as a young woman in her twenties stepped out from one of the bedrooms. Her straight hair was cut bluntly along her chin line, setting off her sharp features. An oversize dress hung loosely on her thin frame.

"You must be the girls from the fan club," the young woman said.

"Hi." Bess extended her hand. "This is Nancy and I'm—"

"Nice to meet you," said the woman as she passed them and went on down the hall.

"I guess that was Roslyn," Nancy said. "She sure didn't seem interested in meeting us." Nancy turned back to the door hidden in the mahogany paneling. "I know there's another way out of there."

"Can it wait until after breakfast?" asked Bess. "I'm starved, and something smells delicious."

"Let's go," said Nancy.

In the dining room Roslyn was standing by the table talking in low tones to the housekeeper, Louise Brewton. A platter of eggs and toast was on the table, next to a large bowl filled with fresh melon and strawberries.

"Breakfast looks wonderful," remarked Nancy.

The two women looked startled to see the girls. Roslyn gave Nancy and Bess a forced smile. "Help yourselves. Louise, would you get two more plates for our guests?"

Without a glance at Nancy and Bess, Louise left the room and quickly returned with the plates. In the daylight Nancy could see that the housekeeper was in her fifties, though her severe expression made her seem older.

"Is it us?" Bess whispered to Nancy. "Or is everyone around here on the grouchy side?"

Nancy smiled and poured some orange juice from the silver pitcher in front of her.

"Isn't Amelia up yet?" Bess asked. It was after nine o'clock.

Roslyn shook her head. "Which is unusual, since . . ." She paused and reached for a basket of muffins.

"Since . . ." Nancy prompted gently.

"Since she's usually up bright and early," Roslyn finished.

"Maybe we should check on her," said Bess, rising from her chair.

"Oh no!" Roslyn replied hastily. Then she flushed. "I mean, Amelia doesn't like to be disturbed when she's in her room."

Bess sat back down, sneaking a look at Nancy.

Nancy took a muffin and slowly buttered it. Why had Roslyn reacted so strongly to Bess?

"Umm." Bess sighed as she finished the eggs on her plate and spooned out a bowl of melon and strawberries. "I could eat like this every day."

Nancy turned to Roslyn. "You're helping Amelia with her writing?"

"Yes, I do most of her typing and some editing." For the first time, Roslyn's face brightened. "She's so talented. I'm learning so much. I'm a writer, too. I hope to be one someday, that is."

"I've read every one of Amelia's books—at least twice!" Bess said enthusiastically.

"Too bad it's taken so long for Amelia's new book to be published. We're dying to read it," Nancy said casually. Roslyn Sillay did indeed seem genuinely concerned about her employer. But still, Nancy wanted to find out what the young woman knew.

"She's still working on it," Roslyn replied hastily. "She hasn't been feeling well and . . ." Roslyn's words trailed off, and then abruptly, she stood up. "Maybe I'd better knock on her door after all." She tossed her napkin on the table and pushed out her chair.

Nancy stood up at the same time. "Ready to go, Bess? I'd like to finish unpacking."

"Sure," said Bess, taking a last bite of muffin. She followed Nancy out of the dining room.

Nancy climbed the stairs right behind Roslyn. She wanted to see for herself that Amelia was okay, but didn't want the secretary to think she was being too nosy. At the top of the stairs, Nancy turned, pretending to enter her own room.

"Amelia?" Roslyn knocked softly on the door. When there was no answer, she rapped louder. A faint groan came from inside.

Nancy couldn't pretend to be uninterested any longer. She rushed past Roslyn and pushed open the door to Amelia's room. The author was still in bed. Her eyes were shut tight, and her face was pale. Nancy hurried to her side.

"Amelia? Are you all right?" Nancy reached for the woman's wrist and felt her pulse. It seemed faint but regular.

"So tired," Amelia mumbled. "And thirsty. Can't get my eyes open." She tried to laugh but coughed instead.

Roslyn dashed into the adjoining bathroom and came out with a glass of water. With Bess's help, Nancy tilted Amelia's head up and gave her a drink.

"How about a cool washcloth to put on her forehead," Nancy suggested.

With a nod, Roslyn went to get one.

"Are you feeling all right?" Nancy asked again.

"Should we call a doctor?" Bess asked anxiously from the other side of the bed.

Amelia shook her head emphatically. "Really,

39

I'm okay. Just couldn't get up. Maybe it was those late hours we kept last night." She winked, and Nancy could see some of her vitality returning.

Roslyn leaned over and laid a damp cloth on Amelia's forehead.

"That's nice. Thank you, all of you." Amelia sank down into the pillow and closed her eyes. Nancy looked up at Roslyn. The young woman's face was ashen.

"Maybe you'd like some tea and a muffin," Roslyn said.

"Breakfast in bed," Amelia said with a smile. "I'd like that."

"Anything to make you feel better." Roslyn patted her employer's hand, then left the room.

"Amelia, are you taking any sleeping medications?" Nancy asked when she was sure Roslyn had gone.

"No. I hate pills. The only thing I take is aspirin, for my arthritis. It was bad last night so I took a couple." She leaned forward and pointed to a nightstand.

Nancy slid open the top drawer. She pulled out a bottle of aspirin, clearly labeled. "May I open it?"

"Of course."

Nancy carefully unscrewed the top and shook out a handful of pills. They were all round and white, but a second glance told her about half were a tiny bit smaller. She read the inscription on the smaller pills, then held them out for Amelia and Bess to see. "These are sleeping pills."

Amelia's eyes grew wide. "What?" She struggled to sit up. "But how did they get in there?"

Nancy frowned. Someone had obviously replaced some of Amelia's aspirin with sleeping pills. Nancy remembered the light in the hallway. Had the person just come from Amelia's room?

"Who has access to your room?" Nancy asked Amelia.

"Why, everyone, I suppose. I don't keep it locked. But I just don't understand. Why would someone want to make me drowsy?"

Just then, Nancy heard footsteps in the hall. Quickly she dropped the pills back into the bottle and put it in the drawer.

Roslyn came into the room, carrying a tray of steaming tea, hot buttered muffins, and a bowl of fresh fruit. "Louise's blueberry muffins," she announced brightly. Amelia sat up, and Bess plumped a pillow behind her.

Roslyn set the tray on her lap. "I'm so glad everything's all right," she said, then looked at Nancy and Bess. "Everything *is* all right, isn't it?" she asked, noticing their serious expressions.

"Oh yes." Amelia nodded vigorously as she took a sip of tea. "I got up last night to greet the girls and must have worn myself out staying up late."

Nancy tried to read Roslyn's face. Did she know

about the sleeping pills? Either she didn't know or she was a great actress, because the only emotion Nancy could see on Roslyn's face was concern.

"Roslyn, be a good girl and start typing a rough draft of the chapter we worked on yesterday," Amelia requested. "I'm feeling much better, and as soon as I dress and show the girls around, I'll be ready to work."

"Are you sure you're up to it?" asked Roslyn.

"Positive. Now, shoo, all of you, and let this old woman have some privacy."

"May we go with Roslyn? I'd love to see where you work," Bess asked eagerly as they stood up.

Good thinking, Bess, Nancy thought. It would give them a reason to tag along after the secretary and do a little snooping.

"I don't know," Roslyn sputtered.

"Just for a minute, until Amelia is ready," Bess said quickly.

"Come on, Roslyn. These are my devoted fans, and they want to get a glimpse of my genius," Amelia said with a twinkle in her eye.

"All right," the secretary reluctantly agreed, and the three girls left Amelia alone and headed downstairs. In the main hall they turned right and went down a long hallway to a door. It opened to a spacious, sunlit office. On one wall, a modern computer was set up. File cabinets flanked both sides. Papers were piled and scattered on every flat surface. Books were stacked on the floor.

42

"Pardon the mess," Roslyn said as she stepped over a box of computer paper. "Amelia has her own system. Believe it or not, she knows where everything is."

The secretary picked up some papers that were clipped together and sat down at the computer.

"What's Amelia working on?" Bess asked. "Or is it a secret?"

Roslyn turned the computer on and let it warm up. "No secret. Her latest historical thriller. The working title is 'Colonial Hero,' but we usually just call it book number twenty-three."

Nancy glanced at the papers. Chapter Two was written on the top sheet. Obviously "book twenty-three" hadn't gotten too far.

Roslyn put a disk into the computer, and soon Chapter Two was on the screen.

"My job is really very simple," she explained. "Amelia dictates the story to me, and I type it into the computer. We print it out and later go over it—sometimes together—and do the first editing."

Bess sighed. She'd been wandering around the office gazing at all the books and papers. "So much for my vision of the writer with her pad and pencil. You know, sipping tea on the wisteria-covered porch while laboring over each sentence."

"Oh, it can be a lot of labor all right," Roslyn muttered. "It seems like Amelia has rewritten the second chapter at least twenty times."

"Really?" Nancy read a paragraph over Roslyn's

43

shoulder. " 'While Amy watched in horror, the men touched the flaming torches to the barn. As if it were a pile of dry kindling, the old building burst into flames. "Where is Lance Mulgrew?" cried Amy.' "

What? Nancy asked silently. She recognized these lines. They were from *Love in Atlanta*. She'd read almost those exact lines just last night.

Nancy looked over to Bess. She was enthusiastically chatting with Roslyn Sillay—who sat absently rapping her pencil on the desk.

"Uh, thanks for the tour," Nancy said. "Bess and I have to go now." She grabbed Bess's arm and hurried her out of the room.

Nancy didn't stop walking until they were at the bottom of the stairwell. "What's the rush?" asked Bess.

"I have to ask you something," said Nancy. "Does Amelia Beaufort use the same characters in more than one book?"

"No, never," replied Bess.

"I didn't think so. I was just double-checking," Nancy told Bess.

"What's going on?" asked Bess.

"Roslyn's not typing a chapter from a new book," Nancy told her. "She's retyping *Love in Atlanta*, which means Amelia's secretary is up to something fishy."

6

Surveying the Grounds

"What are you two whispering about?" boomed a voice at the top of the stairs. Startled, Nancy and Bess looked up. Rex Beaufort was coming down the steps. He was dressed in a sports shirt and slacks.

"We were wondering what to do today," Nancy said without hesitation. "It's going to be beautiful —hot and sunny."

Rex snorted. "You mean muggy and miserable." He wiped his already sweating brow.

"Maybe you could suggest something," Bess said eagerly. "Amelia is showing us around this morning, but then she and Roslyn are going to work."

"My suggestion is you sit on the porch with a cool glass of lemonade and a big fan," Rex answered with a sarcastic grin.

"Do people swim in the Ashley River?" Bess asked.

He shrugged. "It's a little muddy. Do you girls know how to sail?"

Nancy nodded. "I took lessons last summer."

"There you go, then. I've got a boat tied up at the dock. Her sails are on. She's all yours, if you're careful."

"Hey! That sounds like fun!" Bess exclaimed.

"Just don't tip it over," he warned. Then, with a nod, he went out the front door.

Nancy lowered her voice. "A sailboat in the middle of the river will be a great place to finish our discussion. I'm beginning to think even the walls have ears."

Bess's eyes widened as she slowly glanced around the hall. Nancy grinned at her friend's nervous expression.

"Come on, let's go find Amelia," said Bess.

Just then, they heard her voice coming from the dining room.

"Oh, there you are," Amelia said cheerfully as she walked into the hall. She had twisted her gray hair into a knot, and there was now some color in her cheeks. Nancy could see that she felt better.

"How about a tour of the garden before it gets too hot," Amelia suggested as she opened the massive front door.

"Good idea," Bess replied. "It'll be nice to see

46

the place in daylight. The walk up the drive last night was kind of spooky."

Amelia laughed as they stepped onto the porch. Nancy and Bess each took one of her elbows and helped her down the steps.

"Ah, yes," the woman said wistfully. "The moon shining behind the moss-covered trees—it's one of my favorite nighttime scenes. I love to sit on the porch and hear the frogs croaking. So peaceful."

Bess shivered. "I think I like the grounds better in the daytime."

The three paused on the cracked walk and gazed across the front lawn. In the sunlight Nancy could see that last night's impression was right—the grounds hadn't been cared for in a long time.

"As you can see, the last big hurricane did quite a bit of damage." Amelia pointed to several large trees that had fallen. One had been limbed and chopped into firewood. "Miles Brewton, Louise's husband, has made a dent, but there's still so much to do."

"Wasn't the hurricane last fall?" Bess asked.

"Yes. And you should have seen this place. Fortunately, the buildings weathered the storm well."

"What's that building over there?" Nancy pointed toward a two-story, ivy-covered house.

"That's the garage with the old servants' quarters on top. My parents modernized it, and now the Brewtons live there."

47

"It's really neat looking," Bess said. "Everything looks right out of a history book."

Amelia sighed. "The estate was once so magnificent. In the summertime we'd cut gladioli and foxglove and arrange bouquets, and we always had fresh vegetables. Now the yard is an overgrown tangle of weeds. I tried to keep the garden going as long as I could, but then . . ." She stared sadly down at her gnarled fingers. "It just got too painful. And since the last hurricane, I guess I've given up."

"Couldn't you hire someone to help?" Nancy asked.

"I've hired Rex to help Miles this summer, but it's a big job." Amelia chuckled ruefully. "I can see you girls have an exaggerated idea of what writers earn. It costs a fortune to maintain a place like this. Besides, I've been paying Roslyn to help me with my writing, too, and that's about all I can afford."

"Speaking of Roslyn," said Bess, "did you ever get a chance to ask her about mailing the letters to me?"

"Yes," replied Amelia. "She said she mailed them. It's really a mystery."

Bess and Nancy exchanged looks as they crossed some moss-covered flagstones to the side of the house. When they rounded the corner, both girls stopped and gasped.

A garden of rosebushes stretched bright and fragrant before them. They'd been planted in a zigzag so that the white, pink, and red colors

48

alternated. Beyond the flowers, the Ashley River sparkled.

"What a view!" Bess exclaimed.

"We've tried to keep the roses healthy." Amelia hobbled up to a bush and lovingly touched a bright bud. "These bushes once formed a giant M for Magnolia Mansion. The garden has been here since before the Civil War. Can you imagine? My great-grandparents once walked this path."

"That reminds me," Nancy interrupted. "During the war, did your family have hidden stairs built?"

Amelia nodded. "Yes. It was an escape route in case the Yankees attacked."

Nancy told her about the light she'd seen the night before. "I found a door in the paneling, and I wondered where it led," she said, deciding not to tell Amelia that she'd actually been inside the passageway.

"It leads to stairs that go down under the first floor," Amelia told her. "They lead to a trapdoor to the outside. Here, I'll show you." She took the two girls to the back of the mansion and pointed to several thick bushes growing against the house. Nancy dropped to her knees and peered under the lower branches.

A wooden door poked up from the ground. Nancy already knew that it was boarded up on the other side. Parting the branches with her hand, Nancy inspected the area. Cobwebs laced over the rusted hinge, and the dirt and leaves surrounding

49

the door looked as if they hadn't been disturbed in years.

She backed out of the bushes. "Well, whoever used the secret passageway last night didn't come out this way."

"Maybe the person came back into the hallway after we'd gone to bed," Bess said.

"Maybe." Nancy looked doubtful. She stepped back and studied the side of the house. "What room is at this end of the house?"

"The kitchen," Amelia answered promptly. "The stairs in the passageway were built in an old pantry."

"Hmmm," Nancy replied. "That means whoever used those stairs last night could've heard every word we said while we were sitting in the kitchen. It could also be how someone got away after putting the sleeping pills in your aspirin bottle."

Roslyn Sillay suddenly appeared around the corner. Nancy wondered if she'd been hovering on the other side of the house eavesdropping.

"Amelia was just showing us the grounds," Bess said. "What a perfect setting for a writer of gothic novels."

"Speaking of which"—Roslyn linked her arm through Amelia's—"I've finished typing Chapter Two. Are you ready to get to work?"

"Yes. I need to read it over and—"

"No, you don't," Roslyn broke in. "Chapter Two

is perfect. We need to start Chapter Three. Remember, Mr. Stone's going to be here tomorrow and we need to have something to show him."

"Oh, that's right." Amelia chuckled. "My agent's coming to check personally on my progress. Isn't he *sweet*," she added in a joking tone. "You girls have a good time. I'll see you at lunch. Louise serves at one sharp."

"Thanks for the tour," Nancy and Bess chorused. As soon as the other two left, Bess turned to Nancy.

"Boy, is her agent going to be mad when he finds out book number twenty-three is the same as *Love in Atlanta*."

"Not if he hasn't read it. You said it was her first book. Was it very popular?"

Bess thought a second. "Now that you mention it, no."

The two girls began to stroll down the slope to the river. "Which means that if Mr. Stone hasn't read *Love in Atlanta*, he could easily be fooled," Nancy said.

Bess threw her hands in the air. "I don't get it. Do you think Roslyn just had that old chapter in the computer to fool us?"

Nancy shook her head. "No, I don't think so. I think Roslyn really believes she's typing book number twenty-three."

Bess stopped in her tracks. "Which means Amelia . . ." Her voice trailed off.

51

". . . is trying to pull the wool over somebody's eyes," finished Nancy. "But why? I don't think she's telling us everything."

Bess put her hands on her hips. "Do you actually think that sweet old lady is lying? Or worse yet, staging her own accidents?"

Nancy shrugged. "Who knows? I do think that this whole situation is a lot more complicated than we thought. And even worse, if someone was on the secret stairs, listening to our conversation last night, we may have blown our cover."

Bess groaned. "Oh, great. My head's already spinning, trying to keep all the facts straight."

Nancy laughed. "Come on. Let's finish our talk in the privacy of the sailboat." She pointed toward a dock jutting into the river.

"Good idea. Maybe there's a cool breeze out there, too. It sure is hot," Bess added as they headed away from the shade trees and down to the dock.

"Watch your step," Nancy warned. "Some of the planks are rotten."

When they reached the end of the dock, Nancy took off her sandals and jumped into the small sailboat.

"You made that look so easy." Bess grabbed Nancy's hand and jumped in, almost losing her balance.

Nancy began poking around, trying to locate everything they needed. "Here. Slip on this lifejacket," she told Bess. Then she put one on, too.

Soon the girls were sailing out into the river. The wind was so gentle that Nancy let Bess try her hand at controlling the sails.

Once Bess felt fairly confident, Nancy went back to talking about the case. "Right now, Rex is still our number-one suspect. He's the only one with a motive that we know of. But Roslyn is suspect because she didn't mail your letters. And Amelia is writing a phony novel. It's just not coming together."

As Nancy spoke, there was a strong gust of wind from the shore. The mainsail billowed, tilting the boat sideways. "Let the line go slack!" Nancy hollered.

But Bess froze. She held on to the line tightly, her knuckles white with the effort.

At that moment, a loud grinding noise made Nancy look at the boom—the heavy piece of wood across the bottom of the mainsail. Her eyes grew wide with horror. There was a loud crack, and then the boom separated from the upright mast.

Helplessly, Nancy watched the large sail fall.

"We're going over!" she shouted at Bess. In the next second she saw the boom swing toward her. A searing pain exploded in her head as the boom smashed into her. The next thing she knew, she was plummeting into the water.

53

7

Not-So-Smooth Sailing

"Nancy! Nancy!" The sound of Bess's voice broke through Nancy's throbbing headache. Cool waves lapped over her cheeks and into her mouth. She sputtered, then jerked her head out of the water.

"Nancy!" Bess was beside her, shaking her arm. "Are you all right?"

Rubbing her head, Nancy nodded. "I'm glad we put on these life preservers," she said ruefully. The two girls were floating in the water about one hundred feet offshore. The sailboat lay on its side next to them like a wounded sea gull.

"What happened?" Bess asked. "You yelled something, then *wham*, over we went."

"I'm not sure," Nancy said. She slowly made her

way around the boat to where the boom lay floating in the water. One quick glance told her something was terribly wrong, but she'd have to get the boat to shore to find out exactly what.

"You'd better take it easy, Nancy," called Bess. "You were out cold for a second. I was scared to death!"

A powerboat roared past them. Bess waved her hands in the air, trying to get the driver's attention, but he was concentrating on the skier he was towing.

"So much for saving damsels in distress," she muttered.

Nancy rubbed her forehead. Already she could feel a knot forming. "I really cracked my head on the boom."

Bess looked carefully at the bruise. "We have to get you to a doctor as soon as we get ashore."

"It hurts pretty badly," Nancy admitted, "but I think I'll be okay. Hey, there's someone on shore." A man dressed in coveralls with a hat pulled low over his face stood at the end of the dock. "Help!" she called, waving one hand in the air.

The man stared at them a second. Then he turned and walked back to land, disappearing behind the trees.

"Great. Definitely no knights in shining armor around here," Bess grumbled. "I can see we're on our own."

Suddenly they heard the roar of a motor. A small outboard zoomed out from the boathouse. The driver was the man they'd just seen on the dock. He expertly guided the motorboat to the sailboat. Nancy swam to the damaged boat's bow. Without a word, he threw her a rope. She wound it around a cleat on the foredeck of the sailboat.

"Get on his boat," said Bess firmly.

Nancy's head ached so badly that she obeyed.

The man instructed Bess on how to right the boat by leaning on the centerboard, which jutted out from the boat's bottom.

When the boat was right side up, Bess climbed aboard the motorboat. The man towed the sailboat toward shore.

"Thanks," said Nancy, rubbing her head. "Are you Louise's husband, Miles?" The man nodded. "I'm Nancy and this is Bess. And we are very glad to see you."

"Shouldn't go sailing unless you know what you're doing," he said tersely, gazing at them from under his hat brim. His tanned face was leathery and lined with wrinkles. His hands were callused and strong.

"Nancy knows how to sail," Bess defended her friend. "There was something wrong with your boat."

"Rex's boat," Miles grunted. Revving the motor, he drove the outboard into the boathouse.

"Come on, let's find out what went wrong,"

56

Nancy said after Miles had left them alone. "That boom didn't fall off by accident."

"Why don't you lie down up at the house?" Bess suggested.

Nancy's head ached, but she needed to know what had happened. Ignoring Bess's plea, she stepped into the boat and immediately checked the boom, then the gooseneck fitting on the mast. "Just what I thought," she said.

"What? Tell me. I don't have a clue." Bess came up beside her friend.

"The pin that connects the mast to the boom is missing."

"Oh, great. That means it's on the bottom of the river."

Nancy shook her head. "That means someone took the pin out *before* we set sail."

"Run that by me again," said Bess.

"Somebody sabotaged the boat. Fortunately for us, the wind hit the boat when we weren't too far from shore. Otherwise, we'd have capsized in the middle of who knows where."

"But why?" Bess said. "Everybody thinks we're the president and vice president of Amelia's fan club. That's hardly a reason to try to hurt us."

"Right." Nancy frowned. "Which proves that someone *definitely* knows what we're doing here."

"Rex?" asked Bess.

"He was the only one who knew we were going sailing," Nancy pointed out.

"Anybody could've heard us in the hall."

"True." Nancy sighed. "It sure would be nice if we could narrow down the suspects."

"Don't forget we haven't figured out the *motive*." Bess put her hands on her hips.

Nancy chuckled. "You really are getting to be a great detective."

"No. If I were great, I'd have figured out what's going on by now."

"Well, that's what we need to do," Nancy said, despite her throbbing head. "Dig up some hard evidence. So let's get back to the mansion and solve this mystery."

It was cool and quiet back at the house. At Bess's insistence, Nancy took two aspirin and lay down on their soft bed. The mystery could wait at least a little while. In minutes, she was asleep.

When Nancy awoke, she could tell by the sunlight that it was already afternoon. A tray of biscuits, warm fried chicken, and a salad lay on the table beside her. Slowly she raised up on her elbows. The knot on her forehead hurt when she touched it, but the worst of the pain had passed.

"How are you feeling?" asked Bess, sticking her head in the door.

"A lot better," Nancy told her.

"Eat this lunch," Bess ordered. She sat down on the edge of the bed. "That Louise is a sourpuss, but she's a great cook."

58

"Thanks," said Nancy, as Bess put the tray on her lap. "Who's around?" she asked, taking a bite of the chicken.

"Nobody," Bess said. "Amelia is napping, Roslyn is typing, and I saw Rex take the truck out. I don't know where Louise and Miles are, but I don't see them anywhere."

"Great," Nancy said. "It's a perfect time to do some snooping. Let's start with Rex's room."

"Are you sure you feel well enough?"

"I'm okay," Nancy assured her. As soon as she had finished lunch, she kicked off the covers and was out of bed.

"What bedroom did Rex come from this morning?" she asked Bess out in the hallway.

"That one." Bess pointed to the last door across the hallway.

Outside Rex's room, Nancy stopped. "Wait here," she instructed Bess. "If someone comes, act as if you've been admiring the house. Say, 'This is sure a great house.'"

"We won't try rapping this time, huh?" Bess joked.

Nancy smiled. "Nope. I think it has a few problems. This will work better." She turned the doorknob and quietly sneaked into Rex's room.

Nancy tiptoed over to the dresser. She scanned the after-shave, change, and hairbrush that were sitting on top. She wasn't exactly sure what she was looking for. But anything that would tell her more about Rex—or tie him to the mysterious happenings at Magnolia Mansion—would be a big help.

One by one she opened the drawers and gently searched through the neatly folded shirts and pants. Nothing.

It wasn't until she searched the last drawer that Nancy found something that looked like a clue. It was a business card.

RICHARD LEGERE
SOUTH CAROLINA REALTY
Call us for the best real estate deals
in Charleston

"Bingo," Nancy whispered to herself. She slipped the card into her pocket.

"Isn't this a great house!" she heard Bess call from the hallway.

Nancy looked frantically around the room. Oh, great, she thought. There's not even a closet. Maybe Bess's signal meant it was just Roslyn or Louise coming up the stairs.

"Gee, Rex." Bess's voice sounded unnaturally loud. "I have something to tell you about your boat. Don't be too angry. It really wasn't our fault . . ."

Rex! Nancy dove for the floor, hoping to hide under the bed. But it was too high, and the bedspread didn't reach the floor. Rex would see her in an instant.

Just then, she spotted an old wardrobe. She

quickly opened the door and climbed inside, ducking between hangers of shirts and slacks. After shutting the door as best she could, she huddled down in the darkest corner and held her breath.

She could still hear Bess and Rex talking, but their voices were muffled. The next thing she heard was the sound of the bedroom door opening and closing.

She heard Rex's footsteps move across the floor. Nancy covered her mouth, barely daring to breathe. Then the footsteps stopped. A shadow fell along the bottom of the wardrobe door where light had been showing before. Rex was standing right in front of the wardrobe. In a second, he would open the door and find Nancy hiding inside.

8

Suspicious Minds

"Rex!" Nancy heard Bess's voice calling from outside the door.

"Yeah?"

"Phone call. It's the garage calling about your aunt's car," Bess said.

"Be right there."

Nancy sighed with relief. Good move, Bess! she thought thankfully.

As soon as she heard Rex leave the room, she scrambled from the wardrobe and ran out into the hallway.

Bess was waiting outside. "What a close call!" she cried.

"Fast thinking," Nancy commended her friend. "He was just about to discover me. I wonder what he'll think when he gets downstairs and discovers there's no call."

Bess giggled. "It's those phones again. They're always breaking down."

Nancy grabbed her friend's arm and hurried her into their bedroom. "Look what I discovered," she said, producing the business card.

"I don't get it," said Bess, reading the card.

"Why would Rex have a realtor's business card?" Nancy said. "I think innocent nephew Rex is trying to scare poor Aunt Amelia to death. Or at least into a state where she's so rattled that he can have her declared insane. Then Magnolia Mansion would be his."

Bess was silent for a few moments as she took in Nancy's theory. "It certainly fits with what's been happening. Do you think he knows who we are?"

Nancy nodded. "He might. He could have eavesdropped on any one of our conversations with Amelia. It's even possible that he's been intercepting your letters from her."

"You're right," Bess said slowly. "Amelia said that in the last letter she told me she was sending the tickets. Maybe Rex has known about us all along."

"It would explain why the phone line was cut during my conversation with Amelia," Nancy added. "And why Rex would want to scare us away by rigging the boat."

63

"Scare us or put us in the hospital, you mean," said Bess.

"What do we do now?"

"I have a plan," Nancy replied.

That night while everyone was sitting down to dinner, Nancy went to the hall phone. She dialed the number on the business card she'd found in Rex's room.

"Why, Mr. Legere," she said in a southern drawl when the man picked up, "I am so glad you are still in. I desperately need to see you tomorrow. Our newspaper has a column called 'Businessperson of the Month.' We've selected you, but I am so late on my deadline that if I don't see you tomorrow, the feature won't run."

"That's very flattering," said the man. "But to-morrow is a very full—"

"Oh, Mr. Legere," Nancy pleaded, "I will be in such trouble if I don't get this interview. Say you'll help a lady in distress. I do so look forward to meeting you."

The realtor chuckled. "Well, all right, come down. I can probably squeeze you in around eleven."

"Thank you so much, sir. You are a true gentleman. See you at eleven," Nancy said. As she hung up the phone, she felt pleased with her success. Watching *Gone with the Wind* ten times had finally paid off.

"Sorry I'm late for dinner," Nancy called cheerfully as she walked into the dining room. At the table, everyone looked somber.

"What's wrong?" she asked.

Amelia wrung her hands. "After hearing about your boating accident, this seems rather trivial, but I was just asking if anyone had seen my great-grandfather's Confederate uniform. It's usually locked away in a trunk in my room. I went to look at it today—I wanted to check a detail for my book—and discovered it was gone. It has great sentimental value to me, and it's a valuable antique. The uniform was completely intact: hat, belt, sword, everything."

Nancy's mind flashed on the belt buckle she'd found this morning. How did this piece fit into the puzzle? she wondered. She decided to stick to her decision not to tell Amelia about the buckle until she knew more about what was going on at the house.

"That's what happens when you let strangers into your home," Louise Brewton said to Amelia. The woman's dark eyes burned bitterly as she stared at Nancy.

"Louise, that was uncalled for," Amelia scolded. "I wasn't accusing anyone. In the state I've been in lately, I could have done anything with it. I might have told Roslyn to send it to the dry cleaner, for all I know." Amelia's face seemed to cloud with confusion. "I didn't do that, did I?" she asked Roslyn.

Roslyn smiled at Amelia weakly. "No, you didn't."

"I didn't think so," said Amelia, sighing deeply.

The rest of the meal was eaten in silence. Amelia was plainly heartbroken over the loss of the uniform. Louise glared at Nancy and Bess at every opportunity. Rex and Roslyn ate without even looking up.

After dinner, Nancy and Bess took a walk on the grounds. Nancy told her friend about her conversation with Mr. Legere. "Do you think we can fool him?" asked Bess.

"Why, sure, honey," Nancy said in her phony southern accent.

"I guess it takes more than a bump on the head to slow you down," commented Bess.

Nancy touched her forehead gingerly. "Don't remind me. I'm trying not to think about it."

As the boathouse came into view, Nancy checked to see if anyone was nearby. Everything seemed quiet and still. "I want to look in the boathouse a sec," she told Bess.

"What for?" Bess asked.

"Just a hunch," she said.

Inside the boathouse Nancy noticed that the sail on the sailboat had been furled, and the rest of the broken boat had been left in neat condition. Miles must have come back to do this, she mused.

66

"Let's look around," Nancy said to Bess. "If someone did remove the pin before we went sailing, we might find a clue somewhere here in the boathouse."

The two girls covered every inch of the floor, carefully scanning the wide floorboards. They looked behind paddles, old sails, and rusted outboard motors. It seemed hopeless, until Nancy began searching under a pile of life preservers. "Hey, Bess, look at this," Nancy called.

"Did you find a clue?" asked Bess, crossing the boathouse to Nancy.

"Maybe." Nancy pushed back the pile of preservers. Underneath, in the floor, was a rusted metal door. It took all Nancy's strength to pull it up.

Bess and Nancy stared at the dark opening beyond the door. "It's just a hole," said Bess.

"No, it's a passageway," Nancy said, lifting a thick rope that was tied to a metal loop at the side of the opening. She dropped the rope down into the dark hole. "I was always good at rope climbing in gym," she said, grasping the top of the rope.

"Nancy!" Bess cried. "You are not going down there. It's too . . . dark."

But Nancy was already lowering herself into the hole, holding tightly to the rope. The drop to the floor was about six feet. The bottom was dimly illuminated by the fading light from above.

Sticking close to the wall, Nancy made her way along the dark passageway. After she'd gone about ten yards, she came to an abrupt stop. A door blocked her way.

Nancy jiggled the door handle, but it was no use. The door was locked tight. I'll bet this door leads back into the passageway I explored this morning. This is how the person I met in the hall last night escaped, she realized.

She headed back toward the light. When she was just under the open door, she spotted something she'd overlooked. There, lying on the floor, was the boat pin.

Nancy bent down to pick up the pin. Someone threw this pin down here to get rid of it. That meant—as she'd suspected—the boat's overturning that afternoon hadn't been an accident.

9

Hot Property

That night Nancy stayed up late again, reading the rest of *Love in Atlanta.* When she'd finished, she began Amelia's second book, *Dixie Woman.* In the morning, she and Bess asked Amelia if they could borrow the truck, claiming to want to do some sightseeing.

"So you really think you can drive this thing?" Bess asked, frowning at the pickup truck.

"Sure!" Nancy opened the door and climbed briskly into the driver's seat. She was dressed in a light blue suit, stockings, and low-heeled shoes. To her relief, the knot on her forehead had gone down a lot overnight, and now the bruise was barely noticeable.

Bess didn't move.

"Come on, Bess. We've got no choice. Rex has Amelia's sports car," said Nancy.

Still Bess hesitated. "What if it breaks down in the middle of nowhere?"

"Before breakfast, Amelia assured me that Miles had fixed it. Now come on. If we're going to see Mr. Legere we've got to hurry."

Bess climbed in, and soon the truck was rattling down the drive. Bess unfolded a map of Charleston and surrounding areas. Nancy had circled the location of the real estate company. "Take a right at the end of the driveway," Bess told Nancy. "The office is in a shopping center about five miles down the road."

With both hands on the wheel, Nancy steered the clanking truck onto the road.

"So what do we hope to find out?" Bess asked as she folded up the map.

"We want to know if Rex has been talking to Richard Legere about selling Magnolia Mansion. According to Amelia, her estate could be worth millions." Nancy cocked an eyebrow. "Money's always a strong motive for wanting someone out of the picture."

A few minutes later, Bess pointed to the left. "Cooperstone Shopping Center. That's it."

Nancy turned in. They located the office, then parked at the opposite end. Soon they were seated inside South Carolina Realty's air-conditioned building.

Nancy glanced around. The paneled walls were decorated with framed photos of condominium complexes and luxurious waterside homes. Just what Amelia *didn't* want to see happen to her family's estate.

"Mr. Legere will see you now." The secretary showed them into a spacious office. A heavyset man with droopy jowls and thick hair stood up from behind a wide mahogany desk.

For a moment he looked puzzled, then he smiled genially and held out his hand.

"Richard Legere at your service," he said in a southern drawl. "And I assume you are the lady I spoke to last evening. . . ."

Nancy gave his hand a firm shake. "I'm Nancy Drew, and this is Bess Marvin. It was so kind of you to see us. Since you're Businessperson of the Month, we are most interested in hearing your views on the booming real estate market."

"Really." He gestured to two chairs. "Uh, what paper did you say you were with? You girls don't look old enough to be reporters for the Charleston paper." He fixed a suspicious eye on Nancy.

"We're doing an apprenticeship with the *Charleston Journal*. It's for a college course. Our major is business with a minor in journalism," said Nancy. "This article is my very first. If I don't get the story, I'll be thrown out of the program."

"We think it's important to cover all kinds of local businesses," Bess added, imitating Nancy's drawl.

71

"We haven't featured any realtors, so your agency seemed perfect for the column."

"Ah." Mr. Legere folded his hands and relaxed back in his seat. Nancy hoped that meant he'd accepted their explanation.

Bess and she asked him a few general questions about the real estate business. Then Nancy tried to change the topic to more specific properties, hoping the name Magnolia Mansion would come up.

"So what big deals are you and your company cooking up this year?" she asked offhandedly.

"Well, as you girls know from your business courses, the riskier the venture, the greater the potential for financial gain." Propping his elbows on the desk, Mr. Legere grinned like a satisfied cat. Several huge rings twinkled from his pudgy fingers. "Developing properties brings in the big money." He spun around in his swivel chair and tapped on a wall map. "The banks of the Ashley River, the most valuable property around."

Nancy could almost see him lick his lips.

"And I'm about to buy about a hundred acres of prime land."

Bess gasped. Nancy frowned and poked her friend in the ribs.

"Excuse me." Bess faked a cough.

"That's a beautiful area. So many historic homes, though," Nancy said. "It would be a shame to tear them down."

"You don't have to tear them down." Mr. Legere shrugged. "You build around them—condos, golf courses, a conference center. An old mansion makes a great clubhouse."

"I simply can't imagine Magnolia Mansion with a bar, dance floor, and restaurant built into it," said Bess.

Mr. Legere's expression suddenly grew cold. "Enough questions," he said abruptly. He stood, indicating that the interview was over. "I don't know who you girls really are, but you've taken too much of my time already."

Nancy and Bess stood up. "I don't know what you mean," said Nancy rapidly. "But thank you for your time. We'll send you a copy of the article."

Minutes later, Bess and Nancy were back outside. "Boy, he sure got rid of us quick," Bess said. "What tipped him off that we weren't for real?"

"You mentioned Magnolia Mansion," Nancy said. "We weren't supposed to know where he intended to buy."

"Oops." Bess covered her mouth. "At least now we know he's got his eye on Magnolia Mansion."

"Which means he's *got* to be dealing with Rex. Amelia's nephew is the only one who could get legal control of the property."

Bess looked worried. "I just hope we're in time to stop Rex from doing something drastic."

Nancy patted her friend's shoulder. "I think so.

Amelia is a lot tougher than she looks." She sighed. "The hard part is getting something concrete on Rex. He's smart and he's got a lot at stake."

"Yeah. Like a million dollars' worth," added Bess.

Fifteen minutes later, Nancy parked the truck in the mansion's driveway. For a second, both girls sat in silence. Between the heat and the strain of the meeting with Mr. Legere, they felt exhausted.

Finally, Nancy checked her watch. "We've got an hour before lunch. What do you feel like doing?"

"Nothing," said Bess, "except getting out of these clothes and into shorts."

"For once I don't feel like doing much, either," Nancy agreed. "Maybe a little sunbathing on the dock will help us think."

"Great idea. Let's put on our swimsuits and get some of Louise's fresh-squeezed lemonade and chill out."

"You mean, burn up." Nancy laughed. She put her arm through Bess's, and the girls headed for the house.

"Meet you upstairs," Bess said when they reached the kitchen. "I'll get the lemonade right now."

Nancy nodded, and then slipped off her shoes and slowly climbed the stairs. She had a lot to think about. After all, Bess and she couldn't stay at Magnolia Mansion forever and watch out for

Amelia. They had to come up with some answers for their hostess—and fast.

Outside the door of their room, Nancy paused. She heard a soft thump inside. Holding her breath, she inched closer, then swung the door open. Rex stood by the bed, one hand in Bess's makeup case. His mouth dropped open when he saw Nancy.

"Lose something?" she asked.

He flushed bright red. "Uh. No. I . . ." he stammered. Then he closed Bess's makeup case with a sharp snap. "No, as a matter of fact, I was searching through your things." He straightened and glared at her.

Nancy held his gaze. "That's interesting. Is that an old family custom, or are you looking for something in particular? Fan letters? Club news?"

"It does seem odd that you two don't have any club materials in your room," he said sharply. "You and your pal Bess aren't from Aunt Amelia's fan club. Who are you?"

"What makes you think we're not fans?" Nancy demanded. Despite the threatening glare on Rex's face, Nancy refused to step back.

"Let's just say that I have my sources," Rex growled angrily.

"Then why do you think we're here?" asked Nancy.

For a second, he hesitated. Good, Nancy thought.

75

He doesn't know what we're doing at Magnolia Mansion.

"I'm not sure," he said quietly. He took a few steps toward Nancy, a hard look in his eyes. Nancy's heart thumped. "But believe me," Rex continued, grasping her wrist with a strong hand, "I'm going to find out."

10

Secret Agent Man

"What's going on?" Bess demanded from behind Nancy.

Nancy didn't move. She steadily returned Rex's stare.

Rex glanced at Bess, then dropped Nancy's wrist. "Nothing," he said.

Nancy rubbed the skin where he'd twisted her arm. "Rex was going through your makeup case."

"What!" Bess pushed past Nancy and set two glasses of lemonade on the dresser. She went over to her small suitcase and lifted the lid. "Thanks a lot for messing up my things. It's bad enough you tried to *drown* us yesterday."

Rex reached out his foot and kicked shut the

bedroom door. "You two wrecked my boat—now you're accusing me of trying to drown you! That takes it all!"

"Someone rigged that boat to come apart at the first good wind," said Nancy coolly.

"Well, it wasn't me," said Rex. "Now I want to know what you're doing snooping around Magnolia Mansion."

"Snooping!" Bess cried. "In case you forgot, you are in *our* room and were digging through *my* makeup case."

Rex gave her a cold grin. "But you're the ones pretending to be reporters."

Nancy tried to hide her surprise. So Mr. Legere was Rex's "source." That certainly did link the two of them. "Well, your partner lost no time in calling you," she said.

"Partner!" Rex spat out. "Richard Legere called, furious that I had sent two of my friends in to spy on him. He thought I'd sent you to try to find out how much he'd be willing to pay for the place." Rex studied the two girls a moment. "Now, who are you two?"

Nancy walked to the closet and hung up her suit jacket. She was stalling for time. How could she get answers from Rex without telling him the truth?"

"We wanted to find out which real estate agents were pressuring your aunt to sell," Nancy bluffed. "We're just worried about her."

"That's a lie," Rex stated flatly. "I think you two

78

are real estate agents. I think some out-of-state developer is paying you to find out how much money's been offered for the place—in order to make a winning offer."

"Afraid someone is going to cut you out of a big deal?" Nancy asked.

"Little lady—whoever you are—I suggest you get your facts straight before you go around accusing me," snarled Rex. He pulled his wallet from his back pocket. "And before you find yourselves in even more trouble, I recommend you call the number on this card by tonight."

Rex thrust a business card at Nancy and stormed out of the room.

Nancy smiled wryly as she read the card. She handed it to Bess. "It's the number of an airport limousine service. It's Rex's subtle way of telling us to get lost."

At that moment, Amelia knocked on their door once and then stuck her head inside the room. "Girls, I'd like you to come downstairs to meet my agent, Jeremiah Stone." She chuckled mischievously. "You must do me a favor. Convince him that you really are from my fan club. That way he won't be so furious with me about my unfinished book."

Nancy and Bess followed Amelia into the drawing room. Nancy hadn't been in the room before. For a moment, she glanced around. It looked as if time had stood still and she'd stepped back into the 1800s. Shelves filled with books and family me-

mentos stretched to the ceiling on both sides of a beautiful fireplace. A portrait of a dashing Confederate soldier hung over the mantel. A pair of sconces, their candles burning, lighted the picture.

"Bess and Nancy—meet Jeremiah Stone," Amelia said, gesturing toward the small man sitting on an ornate antique couch.

Jeremiah Stone jumped to his feet and held out his hand. "Glad to meet you," he said. He spoke so fast it sounded like one word. "Amelia has told me a lot about your club's support and encouragement."

"Oh yes. We *love* her books," Bess gushed. "And now that I've had a chance to meet her, I'm even more impressed."

"Good. Good." Jeremiah Stone bobbed his head and ran a finger along his thin mustache. "And I'm sure you can't wait until the new book comes out." He shot a meaningful glance at Amelia.

"Jeremiah, you know I've been working as quickly as I can on 'Colonial Hero,'" Amelia said. "Now, how about some lemonade? Lunch will be ready any minute. Louise is fixing your favorite dishes." Amelia gave Jeremiah a charming smile.

He smacked his lips. "Wonderful. It's been ages since I had a good home-cooked meal. Louise should come to New York City and open up a restaurant."

Nancy and Bess sat on a wooden bench opposite the couch while Jeremiah launched into an animated story about all the terrible food he'd eaten in

80

the last month. Nancy was amazed at how smoothly Amelia had gotten around the subject of her book. What would the agent do when he discovered she was only on Chapter Two—of a book that had already been published?

"I wonder what's keeping Louise," Amelia said, after checking her watch about ten minutes later. "She's usually so punctual. Roslyn, dear, will you go see?"

Nancy turned to where Roslyn was sitting in a straight-backed chair. She'd been so quiet, Nancy hadn't realized she was in the room.

"Of course." Roslyn stood up, and with her eyes glued to the floor, she walked out the door.

That's odd, Nancy thought. Why isn't Roslyn acting more cordial? Nancy peered over at Jeremiah. His gaze was following Roslyn out the door— and it wasn't friendly.

"So, Amelia, when will I get to read 'Colonial Hero'?" Jeremiah rubbed his hands together. "You were really excited about the project. And it sounds like a winner."

"Oh, not until later. You know southerners— pleasure before business." Amelia laughed girlishly, then stood up and limped to the fireplace. "Have I introduced you all to Colonel Ashley Beaufort?"

"Excuse me, ladies." The agent stood up. "I think I'll wash up before lunch." He gave a half-bow, then strode from the room.

Amelia sighed with relief. "Threatening to tell the story of my family always chases him away."

"Your great-grandfather looks like a character from one of your books," said Bess. "I know he was a Civil War hero, but I'd love to hear more about what he did."

"Me, too," Nancy chimed in.

"Ashley Beaufort fearlessly led his troops in the last battle—when Charleston fell to the North," Amelia explained. She picked up a framed letter that was on the mantel. "Here's a letter signed by Jefferson Davis, commending him for his bravery. My great-grandfather was also the key person behind a huge smuggling operation."

"Smuggling!" Bess exclaimed. "That sounds dashing, but wasn't it illegal?"

Amelia laughed. "No, dear. Smuggling jewelry and gold to England was the only way the Confederate army could raise money to purchase guns and supplies. My great-grandfather made sure the valuables reached the ships in the harbor. There they were entrusted to a blockade runner who tried to sail past the Union ships."

"That's really exciting," Bess said. "You should write a book about him."

Suddenly Amelia's face turned red, and she began to cough.

Bess sprang to her side. "Are you all right?"

Amelia waved her away. "Fine."

Roslyn appeared in the doorway. "Lunch is ready."

"Oh, good. Will you call Jeremiah?" Amelia asked. "He's upstairs."

Roslyn nodded.

Bess and Nancy escorted Amelia to the dining room. The table was set with sparkling crystal goblets and silver. Salad garnished with asparagus had already been served.

Rex met them at the door. After helping his aunt to her seat, he sat at the head of the table. Nancy tried to catch his eye, but he started shoveling salad into his mouth as if he were starving. Obviously, their confrontation hadn't ruined his appetite.

"Bess and Nancy, I'd like you on my right and left," Amelia said.

Nancy glanced at Roslyn to see if she was feeling slighted by Amelia's request, but the secretary was staring at the doorway. When Jeremiah appeared, she sat down and immediately began eating. Nancy couldn't help but wonder what was going on between the two.

"Ah, Amelia, a beautiful table as always!" Jeremiah spread his arms wide, then pulled out the chair opposite Roslyn.

"You're dining with history." Amelia picked up a goblet and held it up to the light. "This survived the Civil War. My great-grandmother buried all her valuables in the garden so they were spared when the Union troops swept through."

Rex slouched back in his chair. He was finished

with his salad. "So where's the rest of the food?" he asked. "I've got to get back to work."

As if on cue, Louise brought out a covered dish and set it in front of Amelia.

Jeremiah sniffed the air. "Let me guess. It's Louise's specialty, roast duck."

The housekeeper nodded.

Jeremiah smacked his lips. "A perfect choice! Louise, your duck should be written up in *Southern Cuisine*. Or better yet, perhaps we should talk about your writing a cookbook."

Jeremiah turned to smile at the housekeeper. And for the first time Nancy thought she saw a hint of emotion on the woman's stony face.

"Aunt Amelia, I think you prefer to carve," Rex said impatiently.

"Oh yes." Amelia lifted the lid off the platter and her smile froze. On top of the duck was a white rose, its petals dripping with bright red blood.

11

Fictional Clues

Everyone stared in shocked silence at the blood-spattered white flower.

Finally Jeremiah laughed with delight. "What a dramatic touch!" he exclaimed. "Isn't that a scene from one of your books?"

Nancy looked up at Amelia's face. It was as white as the rose.

"Why . . . yes!" the older woman managed to stammer.

Without a word, Louise plunked the cover on the platter and picked it up. "I'll remove the flower, Miss Beaufort," she said in a hushed voice.

"I'll help." Nancy pushed out her chair and followed Louise into the kitchen. Louise set the duck on the counter. She was gripping the handles of the tray so hard her knuckles were white.

"Louise?" Nancy touched her arm. "Are you all right?"

"Who would do a thing like this to Miss Beaufort?" the woman cried, spinning around. "She's such a dear, sweet lady."

Nancy shook her head. "I don't know. But I'd like to find out. May I?" She pointed to the platter.

Louise wrung her hands on her apron, then nodded. Nancy lifted off the cover. Maybe Jeremiah had thought it was a joke, but she knew better. And obviously Louise did, too.

For a second, she studied the flower. Was the red stuff really blood? Closer examination made her decide it wasn't. Some of the red material was drying. Real blood would be turning brown. This was still bright red.

"Ketchup," Nancy said, and Louise nodded in agreement. "Diluted to look like blood."

"But who could've done it?" Louise asked. "I was in the kitchen all morning. Wait a minute— right before I served, Miss Roslyn poked her head in and said I had a phone call."

Nancy pricked up her ears.

"But when I got into the hall, the line was dead."

"Hmm. Thanks for telling me."

"Are you two fixing another whole duck or

what?" Rex stuck his head into the kitchen. "I have to go, and I'm starved."

"Just a second." Nancy plucked the rose from the duck and threw it in the trash. There was no way the flower could lead her to the guilty party. And she didn't want Amelia to see it again. The author was upset enough.

"The meal is probably ruined," Louise complained.

Nancy smiled reassuringly. "It's still hot, and it smells heavenly," she said as she carried the platter into the dining room.

For a second, she surveyed the group at the table. As usual, Rex looked bored. Roslyn was staring at her plate, her cheeks flushed—because of what? Nancy wondered. Had she planted the rose on the duck when Louise answered the phone?

Next, her gaze slid to Jeremiah. He was charming Bess with a story. Amelia was pretending to listen, but Nancy could tell her heart wasn't in it. She just hoped the rest of the meal didn't bring any more surprises.

"Lunch is served," Amelia announced. "Rex, would you carve?"

"Certainly." He sat up straight, and expertly wielding the knife, began to slice the duck. "Anything to get this show on the road."

Nancy sat down. She squeezed Amelia's hand. It was ice cold.

* * *

After lunch, Jeremiah left for his hotel, to make some phone calls, he said. Nancy and Bess invited Amelia to take a walk with them.

"I'm glad you wanted to talk," said Amelia as they headed for the flower garden. "There's something I must tell you. It's about the things that have been going on."

"They're all coming from your books," Nancy finished the woman's thought.

Bess clapped her hand over her mouth in astonishment. "You're right, Nancy! The blood-spattered flower was in *Dixie Woman.* The slashed pages happened in *Hearts on Fire.* And there was a maid in *Southern Belle* who was drugging the heroine's tea. I can't believe I didn't realize that until you said it."

"I started *Dixie Woman* last night," Nancy explained, "and I got to the part about the flower. I just guessed about the rest. Why didn't you tell us earlier, Amelia? You must have realized what was going on."

"I was afraid you'd think I was crazy. And not everything is from the books. The car brakes giving out isn't there," Amelia told them. "And the phone line being cut isn't in any of my books, of course."

"Neither is our sailing accident nor the missing Confederate uniform," added Bess.

A worried scowl crossed Amelia's face. "Are you counting those events in with my strange happenings?"

"Yes," Nancy said. "Amelia, how much do you trust Rex? I mean, really, truly."

"Rex?" Amelia looked puzzled. "Rex is like a son to me. I trust him completely. As I've told you, the only reason I haven't told him the truth about why you're here is that I don't want him to know how worried I am."

Bess and Nancy exchanged glances, then took turns telling Amelia their suspicions about Rex.

Amelia rapped her cane on the ground. "Rex loves this estate. He would never want to sell it."

"Then help us clear him," Nancy urged her. "Call Mr. Legere and find out what's going on."

"All right," said Amelia, turning back toward the mansion. "I'll do it. I need to know, too, for my own peace of mind."

The girls walked Amelia back to her study. "I'll be right back," she said, leaving them in the hall.

A few minutes later, she returned. "Well, Nancy, you were right . . . and wrong," she said mysteriously. "Rex has been wheeling and dealing—but only on five acres at the farthest end of the estate. It seems Mr. Legere is the one with dreams of turning Magnolia Mansion into a country club."

"But why would Rex offer just the five acres?" Bess asked.

Amelia sighed. "Money. He's afraid I'll lose the whole estate if I can't keep up with my bills. But later my nephew and I will have a serious talk, and I'll find out for sure."

"Thank you," Nancy said, giving the woman's arm a pat. "I know that was hard for you."

"But necessary. Now I'm ready for my nap."

"Let me help." Bess linked her arm through Amelia's, and they started up the hall. Nancy hung back a second, trying to put all the pieces together. She couldn't quite decide if the news cleared Rex or not. Maybe at first he was only interested in selling five acres, and then Mr. Legere's offer for the whole estate had been too tempting for him to resist.

"Coming, Nancy?" Bess called from the main hall. "Maybe we can change into our suits and have a swim after all."

"Sounds good." Nancy hurried to catch up with them. As she approached the wide foyer, the tinkle of glass made her glance up. The crystal chandelier hanging from the ceiling was spinning slowly.

With a jolt, Nancy realized what was happening. The cord holding the heavy chandelier was unraveling before her eyes. In a second, the chandelier would crash to the floor. And Bess and Amelia were standing right under it!

12

A Light Search

"Look out!" Nancy cried as she dove for Bess and Amelia. Ramming her shoulder into Bess's, she shoved her friend into Amelia. The force pushed them both toward the front door. Nancy tumbled to the floor and rolled across the rug. With an earsplitting jangle and crash, the chandelier hit the floor, missing her foot by an inch.

"What in the world!" Louise Brewton rushed into the room, drying her hands on her apron. "Miss Beaufort! Are you hurt?"

Bess dashed around the chandelier and knelt by Nancy's side. "Are you okay?"

"Fine," Nancy gasped. "Just got the wind knocked out of me. How about Amelia?"

Bess helped Nancy to her feet. "I'm all right," said the older woman, as she sat against the wall. "Just a bit shaken up. Louise, could you help me to my room?"

As Nancy looked closely at the chandelier, she saw Amelia's cane sticking out from under the broken glass and twisted wires. Bending down, she pulled it out.

Bess shuddered. "That could have been us."

As much as Nancy didn't want to believe it, she knew her friend was right. Whoever was behind the fake blood on the flower and slashed pages in the book was no longer playing games. Bess and Amelia could have been killed.

Angrily, Nancy poked the cane into the pile of broken glass. "Whoever did this means business," she told Bess.

"It could have been an accident," Bess said.

"I don't think so." Nancy studied the ceiling. "I'm going to find out how, and why, the chandelier fell."

"What're you going to do?"

"Find a ladder. Look, why don't you check on Amelia? She was really shaken up."

Bess looked torn. "Okay," she said reluctantly, "but if you need help, let me know."

Nancy headed out the front door and down the drive to the garage. Even in the daylight, the old, ivy-covered building looked like the perfect setting for a horror movie. Inside, the garage smelled damp and musty. Cobwebs clung to every corner and birds chirped from their nests in the rafters.

Nancy let her eyes get used to the dark, then searched for a ladder. In a back corner, propped against the wall, stood an old wooden stepladder.

Nancy ran her finger along one of the rungs, then checked it. There wasn't a trace of dust on the wood. Someone had used it very recently.

A clatter behind her made her jump. Nancy held her breath. In the silence, she heard a footstep.

"Who's there?" she called. "Hello?"

A man's profile suddenly appeared in the light of the doorway.

"Mr. Brewton? Is that you?"

A bulb hanging from the ceiling switched on. Nancy recognized Miles Brewton's leathery face and rumpled work clothes.

"Whew! You scared me." She clutched her chest, trying to calm her racing heart.

"What're you doing in here?" he asked in a suspicious voice.

"Looking for a ladder," Nancy quickly explained. "There was an accident in the main hall. The chandelier fell down."

Miles raised one eyebrow. "Fell? That seems unlikely."

"Really? Why do you say that?"

"Been hanging through fires, earthquakes, and floods," Miles replied. "Besides, I just checked it a month ago."

"But who could've tampered with it?" Nancy asked.

He shrugged. "Don't know that answer." Then he leaned closer, his face an eerie yellow in the dim light. "But there are lots of things around here I don't know about."

"What do you mean?" Nancy edged backward. He spat on the floor near her feet.

"Magnolia Mansion has seen a lot of death. Stands to reason there're some restless souls who haven't found peace."

Nancy's eyes grew wide. Was Miles Brewton talking about ghosts? He sounded like Amelia. "You mean deaths that occurred during the Civil War?"

He nodded, then abruptly changed the subject. "I need to go and check on that chandelier." He hoisted the ladder onto his shoulder and strode out of the garage.

Nancy had to shake her head to make sure she wasn't dreaming. Miles might believe ghosts were at work, but she was sure someone at Magnolia Mansion was responsible for all the spooky accidents.

When Nancy caught up to Miles, he was already climbing the porch steps. She leaped up them by twos, then held open the front door.

Five minutes later, he was staring at her from the ladder's top rung. "Nope, I was wrong. This here cord just rusted through. I'll take care of the mess," he added as he climbed down.

* * *

94

That night, Nancy lay in bed unable to sleep. Bess was huddled on her side, rereading Amelia's sixth book, *Carolina Kate.*

With a sigh, Nancy turned toward the window, hoping the breeze might cool her off. But she knew it wasn't only the sticky heat that was keeping her awake.

"I still don't think it was an accident," she said.

"Hmmm?" Bess didn't take her eyes off the book.

"The chandelier. It was too much of a coincidence. That wire had to have been cut."

"Umm."

"Bess, are you listening?" Nancy asked over her shoulder.

Bess stuck her finger in the book to mark her place and looked up. "Nancy, we've been over this a million times. Even if the wire was cut, we still don't know who did it and why. Maybe we'll have some new ideas in the morning." Slumping back against her pillow, she yawned.

"You're right." Nancy shifted, trying to get comfortable. "A good night's sleep will help clear my brain."

"Um. That sounds better." Bess set her book on the nightstand and turned out the light.

Nancy shut her eyes and forced her mind to go blank. She really was tired, and the breeze coming in through the window felt great.

"There is one thing, though," Bess said, sitting up in bed. "When I went to check on Amelia, she

95

wanted me to stay for a minute while she fell asleep."

"Yeah." Nancy yawned.

"And as she drifted off, she kept mumbling things about a book that had to be kept secret."

Nancy's eyelids popped open. "The book she's working on now? 'Colonial Hero' or whatever she called it?"

"Well, that's what I couldn't figure out. I mean, as far as we know, the only book Amelia and Roslyn are working on is a rehash of the one she wrote years ago."

Nancy sat up next to Bess. "Maybe she was talking about not letting anyone know she's reworking the old book. Or, maybe"—Nancy paused —"she's working on another book."

"But why? Why would she need to keep it a secret? And what would it have to do with all the weird things that have happened?"

Nancy leaned over her friend and switched on the light. "Good questions. She must be worried about something if she's talking in her sleep. If we can find a manuscript or notes or *something*, we can figure out exactly what she is working on."

Bess groaned. "Not more snooping."

Nancy swung her legs over the bed. "Come on. I'll need you to help search that rat's nest Amelia calls her office."

She tossed Bess her bathrobe, then slipped on her own.

"Nancy, I really don't want to do this," Bess grumbled. But she was already out of bed with her robe on.

Nancy opened the door into the hall and looked out. It was dark and empty, and there were no cracks of light under anyone's door. She tiptoed from the room with Bess sticking close behind her.

The moonlight through the front windows cast eerie shadows on the walls. Bess gripped Nancy's arm.

The door to Amelia's office was unlocked. As Nancy pushed it open, the rusty hinges creaked. So much for sneaking in quietly, she thought.

Bess quickly shut the door behind them and the girls held their breath. Except for the wind banging the shutters, the house was silent.

Nancy clicked on her small pocket flashlight, then picked her way over the stacks of junk by the window. When she opened the curtains, moonlight streamed in, making it easier to see.

"So what're we hunting for?" Bess asked. She was standing by the desk, poking through a pile of loose papers.

"I'm not sure," Nancy admitted. She bent down and began rummaging through a box at her feet. "Any notes or papers that look important, I guess."

"Most of this stuff looks like junk mail and articles copied from a magazine," Bess said, going through a pile of things on Amelia's desk.

"This is strange," Nancy said, holding up a few

97

pages of handwritten notes. "Amelia *says* she's working on a book about colonial times. But all this stuff in the box is about the Civil War."

"That doesn't prove anything. There's a pile of books on her desk about ships. And several on pirates. Amelia does so much research, she'd need books on everything."

Nancy put Amelia's notes back in the box. "You're right. This is a wild goose chase. I think we need to confront Amelia and find out what's going on."

"Well, let's not give up quite yet." Bess pulled open a file drawer. Nancy laughed. "Boy, that's a switch. For somebody who didn't want to come down here a few minutes ago, you sure seem enthusiastic."

"Hey, we got past all the spooks and shadows. This is the fun stuff—nosing through other people's things." She handed Nancy a folder. "Here, why don't you take a look in this."

The top tab read Contracts.

Nancy leafed through until she found the contract from Amelia's publisher concerning her latest book.

"Hold everything, Bess. This contract says Amelia should be writing a *nonfiction* book about the Civil War. And it's titled 'Charleston Hero,' not 'Colonial Hero.'"

"Are you sure?"

98

Nancy checked the date. "Positive. The first ten chapters were due several weeks ago."

Bess whistled. "No wonder Jeremiah's getting antsy."

Nancy quickly scanned the contract. Attached to it by a paper clip was a letter from Amelia's publisher. "Hey, look at this," Nancy said excitedly. "According to this letter, Amelia's new book was supposed to be a total secret. No one, not even Jeremiah, was supposed to know that Amelia was working on a *nonfiction* book."

Bess took the letter from Nancy. "Let me see that."

"Has Amelia ever said *anything* to you about writing a nonfiction book?" Nancy asked.

Bess thought for a second. "Well, now that you mention it, in one of her letters she mentioned an exciting project she had been researching. But that's all she said."

"How long ago was that?"

"Oh gosh, at least six, seven months ago," Bess recalled.

Nancy looked at the date on top of the contract. "This was signed about a year ago. It must have been what Amelia was working on when she wrote you."

"Do you think Amelia started the book, then stopped for some reason?"

Nancy carefully put the contract and letter back

into the file and handed it to Bess. "Maybe. Unless she still *is* working on the Civil War book but doesn't want anyone—including us—to know."

Bess shrugged and stuck the file back in the cabinet and closed the drawer. "None of this makes any sense to me."

"Maybe things will clear up when we tell Amelia what we found and ask her what's going on," replied Nancy.

"Ugh. I don't look forward to that. What will we say? 'Gee, Amelia, we just happened to be snooping through your things and we found—'"

"Hold on, Bess," Nancy interrupted. She aimed her flashlight at the floor under Roslyn's desk. A small red splotch stained the carpet.

"Looks like blood," Bess observed, coming to Nancy's side.

Nancy knelt and scratched the stain. "It's ketchup," she said. "And it's a new stain. Maybe Roslyn was making bloodstained flowers today instead of typing." Nancy tried the secretary's desk drawer, but it was locked. Then she spied Amelia's plastic long-distance phone card sitting on a pile of papers near her phone. "This will do the trick."

In a flash, Nancy had used the plastic card to push aside the desk's flimsy lock. She pulled open the drawer.

"There's the ketchup," said Bess, picking three plastic packets of fast-food ketchup from the drawer. "But it doesn't really prove anything."

100

Nancy was still rifling through the drawer. She took out an envelope addressed to Roslyn that was postmarked a few months ago. Inside was a letter from Jeremiah Stone. "Roslyn, How is our little scheme working? Please give me an update. Your next payment depends on it. J."

Nancy handed Bess the letter and continued to search under papers in Roslyn's drawer. "Wow!" said Bess. "Looks like Rex has company on the suspect list."

"He sure does," Nancy agreed. She handed Bess three white envelopes. "Look what I just found."

Bess read the address on the envelopes. "My letters!" she cried. "These are the letters Amelia wrote to me. Roslyn never mailed them. They're unopened, so I guess she didn't read them at least."

Suddenly, the door flew open and the light was switched on. "What's going on here?"

Bess and Nancy jumped. Louise Brewton was standing in the doorway, glaring at them. If looks could kill, thought Nancy, we'd both be dead.

13

Rex's Change of Heart

"Oh boy," Bess whispered to Nancy. "Get us out of this one."

"Hi, Louise," Nancy said casually. "Sorry if we were making too much noise. We were just looking through Amelia's things to get some biographical material."

Louise's expression didn't soften. "It's awfully late. And why is the light off?"

"We didn't want to wake anyone up," Bess chimed in.

The stony look on the housekeeper's face told Nancy that Louise didn't believe a word they'd said.

"Ms. Beaufort will hear about this tomorrow!" she stated in her flat voice.

"Oh, she knows already," Nancy fibbed. "She doesn't like us in here when Roslyn's working, so tonight was the first chance we had."

Louise's gaze flickered up and down, noting their pajamas. Then she gestured toward the door. "Good night. I'll lock up."

"Good night," Bess and Nancy chorused as they hurried past her and down the hall. Once they were back in their room, they sat on the bed looking at each other.

"Close call," Bess remarked. "I don't think Louise bought one word we said."

Nancy nodded. "We're going to have to get to Amelia first thing tomorrow and tell her what we were doing in her office."

Nancy sighed as they climbed back into bed and turned out the light.

"One thing's for sure. This is one of the strangest cases we've ever been on."

"Amelia, we need to speak to you," Nancy said to the woman the next morning after they'd eaten.

They'd just finished a delicious breakfast of fruit-filled crepes. Jeremiah and Roslyn were on the porch finishing their coffee. Rex had disappeared into the drawing room.

"Not now." Amelia patted Nancy's arm. "I promised myself I'd speak to my nephew first thing this morning. He's waiting for me now."

"All right, then as soon as you get the chance."

103

Nancy watched anxiously as Amelia slowly made her way to the drawing room and drew the doors shut behind her.

"Well, Miss Drew, why not join us on the porch." Jeremiah came up behind her. He was carrying a steaming pot of coffee. "It's lovely outside this early in the morning."

Nancy glanced up the stairs. Bess had gone to the room to finish blow-drying her hair. Nancy could hear the whir of the dryer.

"Sure." Nancy followed him out the door. Roslyn was seated on a wicker love seat. Her back was stiff as she sipped her coffee and gazed across the gardens.

Jeremiah gestured to an extra cup. "Would you like coffee?"

"No, thank you." Nancy sat in the rocker.

"Tell me, which of Amelia's books are your favorites?" Jeremiah sat back in a cushioned chair, his sharp eyes studying her.

"Oh, I'd say *Dixie Woman* and *Love in Atlanta*," Nancy replied, hoping he wouldn't ask her anything specific about any of the others.

"*Love in Atlanta?*" Jeremiah frowned. "I've been Amelia's agent for years, but I've never read her first book. It was published before she had an agent."

"You must be excited about her latest book," Nancy said.

"Oh yes, if they'd ever let me see it." He looked

over at Roslyn. "But the author and her secretary have been quite elusive. Isn't that so, Miss Sillay?"

Roslyn's fingers clutched her cup tightly. "You'll have to discuss that with Amelia, Mr. Stone. I'm only her employee."

"Hmmph." Looking annoyed, Jeremiah turned back toward Nancy.

"Amelia told me you recommended Roslyn to her," said Nancy. "It seems as if she's been a big help."

Jeremiah nodded curtly. "It seems that way, but I have my doubts."

Roslyn snapped her head around. "I've done all I could!" she retorted. Getting up, she marched angrily into the house, almost running into Bess on the way in.

"Whoa, what was that all about?" Bess said as she stepped onto the porch.

Jeremiah set his cup down with a loud clatter. "Who knows? If you'll excuse me, *some* people have work to do." He stood up and followed the secretary into the house.

"Work on Saturday? No way," Bess said as she sat down. "This is supposed to be a day for swimming, sailing, shopping—"

"And sightseeing," a deep voice said from the front doorway.

They looked up. Rex towered above them, jingling his car keys in his hand.

"Amelia said I should drive you girls into

Charleston. I've got to do some errands, so it'll be on my way."

"But we have to talk to your aunt," Nancy said. She peered up at him, wondering how he'd reacted to Amelia's accusations and if it was safe to take a ride with him. But his face was unreadable.

He shook his head. "I think she needs to discuss some things with Mr. Stone."

Boy, does she, Nancy thought, hoping they could get to Amelia before Louise filled her in on what had happened the night before.

Rex cleared his throat. "I owe you an apology," he said. "You girls brought something out in the open that needed to be discussed."

"You mean the real estate deal," Bess said.

"Yes. My aunt's avoided talking about money— or the lack of it—for so long that I gave up trying to discuss it. So you two were right. I went behind her back, which I never should have done."

Bess nodded. "It did make us suspicious of you, especially after we caught you going through our things."

Rex chuckled. "Now do you trust me enough to take a ride into town? We can continue talking in the car."

Nancy and Bess nodded, and soon they were in Amelia's car, with Rex driving toward Charleston.

"So why were you trying to sell off the five acres?" Nancy asked.

"Money. But not for myself. The mansion's falling

down, the garden looks like a jungle. Aunt Amelia made some foolish investments, and she also owes back taxes. The only thing holding the place together is Miles and Louise Brewton. Why they stay, I'll never know. Amelia doesn't pay them much. And Richard Legere was going to give me almost a hundred thousand dollars for those five acres," Rex explained.

"Wow! That's a lot of money!" cried Bess.

Rex snorted. "He'd make ten times that much developing it."

"Why is Amelia so reluctant to talk about selling?" Nancy asked. "Seems like a good deal to me."

"Well, a while ago she put me off by saying her new book was going to be a best-seller. She seemed so sure, I kind of dropped it. Then"—he shrugged—"I don't know what happened. She got kind of paranoid."

Probably around the same time the accidents and pranks began, Nancy thought. For the first time since they'd driven off, she relaxed. Everything that Rex said made sense.

He screeched to a halt in front of a stop signal. "A couple more blocks and I'll drop you off in the historic district," he said.

"Can I ask you a question?" said Nancy. "Why have you been so rude to us? And why are you being so much friendlier today?"

Rex grinned. "Because Aunt Amelia told me who you two really are," he said. "You don't know how much I detest the members of her fan club. They come to the mansion, eat her food, distract her from her work, steal little odds and ends as souvenirs. But every six months or so, Aunt Amelia lets one or two come for a visit. Then, when I thought you were real estate agents, I hated you even more."

"Who did Amelia say we were?" Nancy asked cautiously.

"She said you were friends whom she invited down to snoop around. It's Aunt Amelia's form of writer's block. When she doesn't want to work, she finds excuses to waste time."

"Then you don't think your aunt has any reason to be worried?" asked Bess from the backseat.

"Aunt Amelia is overly dramatic," said Rex. "That's what makes her such a good writer, but she's always been a little eccentric."

"What about the bloody rose yesterday?" asked Nancy.

Rex shrugged. "I wouldn't be surprised if Aunt Amelia did that herself, as Jeremiah said. She's behind in her work on the new book, and she's trying to throw Stone a curve so he won't bug her about it."

Nancy decided not to say any more. She still wasn't 100 percent sure of Rex, and she didn't want to give too much away.

Rex pulled over to the curb, and Nancy and Bess got out of the car.

"How about if I meet you at the Charleston House Hotel for a late lunch, say one-thirty?" he called out the open car door. Then, slamming it shut, he pulled out into heavy traffic.

"Where's that?" Bess shouted, but her words were lost in the roar of the engine. "I guess the address will be in my guidebook," Bess muttered.

"He sure has done a turnaround," Nancy commented. "I wonder if he's telling us all he knows."

"Nancy, let's forget about him and Magnolia Mansion and everything for one afternoon," said Bess. "I want to be a regular old tourist right now."

Nancy laughed. "Come on, fearless tourist, let's see the sights before it gets too hot."

Bess opened her guidebook to a map, and they figured out where they were. While they were reading, a horse-drawn carriage rolled past.

"That looks like fun. How about a quick walk through one of the historic homes, then a surrey tour?" Bess suggested. "Then we can hit the air-conditioned museum."

"Good plan," Nancy agreed.

They headed for the Joseph Manigault House, a beautiful home built in 1803. It was expertly restored and decorated with antiques. Nancy was intrigued to see it even had a secret stairway between the third and fourth floors.

When they stepped back outside, the bright sun hit them full force.

"Now I see what Magnolia Mansion *could* look like," Nancy said as they walked down the sidewalk.

"Yeah. Wow! Is it hot!" Bess stooped and rubbed the back of her heel. "And boy, do my feet hurt. Let's find that surrey."

"Okay," agreed Nancy. "Where do we get one?"

Bess pointed to the map. "The Charleston Carriage Company's about four blocks from here. We'll have to walk."

Bess's anguished look made Nancy laugh. "The walk will do you good. And if we see a café on the way, I'll treat you to a soda."

The girls started down the street, stopping at the curb to wait for a light. A carriage pulled up in front of them. Calling, "Whoa," the driver halted the chestnut horse.

"Would you like a ride?" he asked. He was dressed in a Confederate uniform. A heavy beard and bushy eyebrows masked his face. Something about his voice sounded familiar to Nancy. But that was impossible, so Nancy decided she was wrong.

"Boy, you came at the right time." Bess climbed in without further encouragement.

"How much?" Nancy asked.

"Five dollars, and worth it on such a hot day."

"Come on, Nancy, get in," Bess said, patting the cushion on the seat. "This is the way to travel."

Nancy paid the man and climbed up next to Bess. The driver clucked to the horse, who took off at a brisk trot. They clip-clopped past cars stuck in traffic and weary-looking walkers.

"Isn't this fun?" Bess giggled.

The driver turned down a cobblestone lane. Tourists dotted the sidewalk, and old homes painted in soft pastels lined the street. The smell of roses and magnolias drifted in from small gardens.

"This is so quaint," Nancy said. "And I've never seen such decorative wrought-iron fences."

Bess opened her guidebook. "The book says that Charleston has so many old gates it's known as the City of Famous Gateways."

She tapped the driver on the shoulder. "Could you tell us a little about this area?"

He grunted, then picking up a buggy whip, he snapped it over the horse. The startled chestnut leapt forward, tossing the girls roughly against the back of their seat.

Nancy grabbed the side of the carriage and pulled herself upright. The driver cracked the whip again, and then in one quick movement, he jumped from the carriage and ran down an alley.

"Hey!" Nancy cried after his fleeing shape. What was going on?

The driverless horse broke into a canter. The surrey bumped and rattled over the cobblestones.

111

Nancy swayed against Bess, knocking her friend sideways.

She grabbed Bess's arm to keep her from falling. Then she looked ahead. The frightened horse was bolting wildly—right toward a busy intersection!

14

The Mystery Driver

"Whoa. Easy!" Nancy called in a soothing voice, though her heart was beating rapidly. She had to stop the horse before it hit a car or caused an accident.

Trying to keep her balance, she pulled herself to a standing position. She had to get the reins—fast!

Nancy tumbled into the driver's seat. Quickly, she reached down, snatching up both reins.

"Whoa," she cried as she pulled on the reins. The horse threw his head up and plunged ahead. A car screeched on its brakes. Another driver honked, frightening the horse even more.

Nancy began to panic. Then out of the corner of her eye, she saw an empty alley—the last before the main road.

Tugging on the right rein with all her strength, she turned the horse toward the alley. As the horse responded, the carriage tilted on two wheels. Bess shrieked and Nancy held her breath, hoping it wouldn't topple sideways.

"Whoa," she called again. "Easy." Straight ahead, at the end of the alley, was a brick wall. Nancy gasped and gave one last pull on the reins. The tired horse slowed to a trot, then, with a shudder, halted several feet in front of the wall.

Exhausted, Nancy slumped in the seat. Her arms ached and her hands were raw from the friction of the leather reins. Bess reached over from behind and hugged her.

"You did it!" she said with a muffled sob. Two men ran up to ask how they were, and a young woman grabbed the horse's bridle. Seconds later, Nancy could hear the blare of a police siren.

Someone helped them from the carriage.

"I don't think I'll ever take a buggy ride again," Bess said with a tired grin.

A handsome police officer strode up, pad in hand. His face looked serious, but there was a twinkle in his eye. "Uh, can I see your driver's license?" he asked Nancy.

When he saw the stunned expression on her face, he grinned. "Just kidding. And don't worry. The real driver already called in and told the dispatcher his carriage had been stolen. That guy rode off with

114

the carriage while the driver was taking a break. I just need you girls to answer some questions."

Nancy launched into a detailed account of the morning as the officer took notes.

"What did the driver look like?" he asked.

When Bess described the uniform and beard, he sighed. "That'll make identification almost impossible. The uniform and the beard, well, you can get them at any tourist shop or costume store."

Nancy nodded. "I thought so. And he didn't say much—though he had a Southern accent."

"Along with everyone else in Charleston." Next the officer asked them their names and where they were staying. "Just in case we catch somebody, though . . ."

"We won't hold our breath," Nancy told him.

"Right. Especially if the carriage company doesn't pursue it. After all, they're getting their horse and buggy back." He shook his head, looking bewildered. "Do you have any idea why the driver jumped ship?"

Nancy shot Bess a warning glance. She didn't want the officer to know about the trouble at Magnolia Mansion. It wasn't police business—yet.

"No. Maybe it was a prank," Bess replied lightly.

"A dangerous one, if you ask me. Can I drop you girls somewhere?" He stuck his pad in his shirt pocket.

Nancy checked her watch. It was almost noon.

"We're supposed to meet a friend at the Charleston House Hotel at one-thirty."

"And believe me, we're not hailing a carriage," Bess joked.

"How about if I drop you off in Battery Park? It's not far from the hotel, and it'll give you a chance to see the city—at a slower pace."

The three laughed. Another policeman had arrived with the owner of the carriage, so Nancy knew the horse was in good hands. With a sigh of relief, she shut the squad car door.

Closing her eyes, she leaned her head back against the seat. Immediately her mind began replaying the whole incident. Who had set up the "accident" and why? Had she been right about the driver's voice? Was he really someone they knew disguised behind that beard?

She knew the driver wasn't Rex. The man had been too short and stocky. But that didn't mean Amelia's nephew hadn't hired someone.

But why stage the whole thing in town? If he'd wanted to get rid of them, he could have done it more easily at the mansion.

Then it dawned on her.

"Miss Drew?" The officer's voice cut into her thoughts. "We're here."

Nancy sat up and blinked. Bess was standing outside the squad car, looking at her through the window.

116

"Are you all right?" she asked after Nancy thanked the officer and climbed out.

Shutting the car door, Nancy pulled Bess away from the curb and into the park. "I just figured out why the driver seemed so familiar."

"Why?" asked Bess.

"He was the same build as Miles Brewton," Nancy explained excitedly. "And his voice sounded like Miles's, too."

Bess looked doubtful. "I don't know, Nancy," she said, sinking onto a park bench. "I don't get it— why would Miles go to such great lengths to try to hurt us?"

"I think it was to distract us from what's happening at Magnolia Mansion and make it seem as if the incidents aren't just connected to Amelia. It's pretty clear that whoever was driving the carriage wanted to scare us."

"He succeeded in scaring me!" Bess exclaimed, rubbing her arm where she'd bounced against the back of the carriage.

Nancy looked around. "Come on, let's find a phone and call Magnolia Mansion. I'll find out if Miles is home."

Dragging Bess with her, Nancy crossed the street to a small coffee shop.

"Ah, food," Bess said. "I'm starved." She sat down at a table and ordered sodas and some pastries while Nancy used the phone.

"Well?" Bess asked when her friend returned.

Nancy sat down and broke off a piece of one of the pastries. "I talked to Louise and pretended we might need a ride back. She said Amelia, Jeremiah, and Roslyn were still working, and Miles was out in the garden. I didn't say anything about the accident."

Bess raised her eyebrows. "So maybe it wasn't Miles driving the carriage."

Nancy tapped the table with a spoon. "I don't know *what* to think. Louise made it sound as if Miles was available. She said to call if we needed a ride, so I guess that clears him. How long before we meet Rex?"

Bess checked her watch. "An hour. I'm glad I ate something now," she said gloomily. "I can tell that lunch is going to be more like a police interrogation."

Nancy laughed. "Probably. But I promise I won't be too rough on him. Come on. Finish your soda. Let's enjoy Charleston while we can."

The Charleston House Hotel was cool and elegant. The girls were escorted into the hushed interior of the restaurant by a maître d' in a starched uniform. Nancy scanned the room, happy to note that many other patrons looked as if they were from out of town.

Rex waved from a table. The maître d' seated

them as carefully as if they were wearing formal gowns, handed them a menu, and then, with a bow, moved away.

"Well, weary sightseers, did you enjoy our lovely town?" Rex asked.

"A real blast," Bess mumbled.

Rex gave her a puzzled look, then pointed to several entries on the menu. "This place is known for the deviled crab and for the shrimp salad."

"Yum." Bess licked her lips. "I'll take one of each."

Rex laughed. "Go ahead. It's my treat."

"That's not necessary," Nancy said quickly.

"Hey, you've been a big help to my aunt. She likes having you around. It's the least I can do," he replied gallantly.

They ordered. Rex and Bess talked about the sights they'd seen that morning. Nancy folded and unfolded her napkin, wondering if Rex had somehow been involved in the carriage accident. So far, his actions and words hadn't told her anything.

"How was your morning?" she asked him.

"Boring. I went to the hardware store, then off to the nursery for weed killer."

"Oh, good, so you weren't the one driving the carriage," Bess blurted out.

Nancy kicked her under the table.

Rex sat back in his chair, giving Bess a curious look.

119

Just then the waiter came up with a pitcher of water and a basket of hot popovers. Nancy was glad for the interruption.

"*Now* what are you accusing me of?" Rex demanded as soon as the waiter had left. Bess busily buttered a popover.

Nancy decided to plunge in and tell him the whole story, leaving out only her suspicions about Miles. While she talked, she watched Rex's expression carefully. All she saw was sincere interest.

As Nancy finished telling Rex about the incident, the waiter returned with the main course.

"This looks great!" Bess scooped up a forkful of shrimp salad. Nancy had ordered the deviled crab, and it looked wonderful.

The three ate in hungry silence. Finally Rex set down his fork and gave a satisfied sigh.

"That's some story you told," he said. "I'm glad to see you girls are okay. Now, are you up to some detective work?"

"Detective work?" Nancy and Bess said together.

"Of course!" Rex sat forward eagerly. "We need to go back to the scene of the crime and look for clues." He signaled for the waiter.

"Great idea," Nancy responded eagerly. "The police won't bother. I mean, they have more important cases than a runaway horse." Secretly she was thinking it would give her a chance to observe Rex. She was pretty confident they could trust Amelia's nephew, but she wasn't absolutely certain.

The girls quickly located the alley down which the man had disappeared. Rex pulled the car in, parked under a sign that said Towaway Zone, and the three jumped out.

"So what are we searching for?" Bess grumbled as she looked around at all the bags of garbage.

"Anything that'll give us a clue as to the identity of the driver." Nancy was already rummaging in a trash can.

"Anything that'll clear *me*," Rex added. "I'm sick of being the bad guy."

Wrinkling her nose, Bess poked halfheartedly at a box of old cans. "But this stuff smells." She held her nose and turned over a rusty can. Her finger touched something furry. "*Eiii!*" she screeched, jumping backward onto Nancy's toes.

"Ouch!" Nancy hopped on one foot.

Bess gestured toward the box. "There's some kind of—of—creature in there."

"Oh, come on, Bess. It's probably a mouse." Nancy peered into the box. "Hey!" She grabbed a stick, fished under the cans, and pulled out what had scared Bess.

"The driver's beard!" Bess exclaimed.

"Yeah. We can drop it off at the police station, though my hunch is it won't do us much good. Looks like a costume-type beard you could buy anywhere," said Nancy.

"Hey!" Rex called from halfway down the alley. "Come look at this."

The girls took off at a jog. Rex was standing by a picket fence. He pointed to a footprint in the soft mud on the other side. "The driver must've escaped over the fence and through this backyard. It's a blind alley and there's no other way out."

"Boy, he sure wasn't careful about not leaving clues behind, was he?" Bess commented.

"That's for sure. Look at this." Leaning over the fence, Nancy used her stick to poke at something under a rosebush. She speared it, then carefully raised it up so everyone could see. It was a Confederate hat.

"He was definitely in a hurry," Bess said. "Or didn't think anyone would come back and look for evidence."

Rex stepped closer and studied the hat. "Well, whatever his reason, he made a big mistake, because this just might help the police track the driver."

"Why do you say that?" Nancy asked.

"Because this hat isn't from a costume shop or dime store. It's a genuine Confederate cap."

"How do you know?" asked Nancy.

"It's exactly like the one Aunt Amelia seems to think she's missing." Rex's eyes narrowed and he looked inside the cap. The initials AB were stitched in the lining.

"Ashley Beaufort!" Nancy cried. "It *is* the hat from Amelia's missing uniform!"

122

15

Clues in the Kitchen

Nancy was quiet on the way home. She now knew for certain that someone staying at Magnolia Mansion was responsible for the surrey accident. The phony driver had seemed so much like Miles. But she couldn't prove it. And what was his motive?

Rex pulled up in front of the mansion. Bess and Nancy thanked him for his help and got out. Eager to find Amelia, the girls dashed up the steps and through the front door. Inside the house an angry voice was coming from the drawing room. Nancy stopped in her tracks, listening.

It was Roslyn.

"It sounds as if she's crying," whispered Bess.

Rex rushed in behind them, almost knocking the

123

girls over. Nancy quickly put a finger to her lips to silence him.

"I've had enough, Jeremiah!" Roslyn's voice rose, and they could hear her clearly. "You've bribed me for the last time!"

Bess gasped at the young woman's words. Nancy hushed her friend, then tiptoed to the closed drawing-room doors. She put her ear to the crack.

"You're in too deep to get out now," Jeremiah said in a low tone. "Do you hear me?"

"Just watch me!"

Nancy heard the scrape of a chair being pushed back, then footsteps. Suddenly, the doors flew open. Roslyn screamed at the sight of the three staring faces.

Jeremiah jumped up from the couch, his cheeks bright red. "What—what're you doing listening at the door!" he sputtered.

"Protecting Amelia!" Nancy said.

"From people who are supposed to be her friends!" Bess chimed in.

Rex pushed his way into the room. "Maybe you two had better explain what's going on," he said angrily. "Or pack your bags and get out."

Putting her hands in front of her face, Roslyn began to sob.

"Oh, hush," Jeremiah said impatiently. Sitting down, he crossed his legs. "We haven't done anything wrong."

124

"Oh, really?" Nancy strode in and sat opposite him. "Then why would you have to bribe Roslyn?"

Jeremiah looked disgusted. "Because she's such a mouse. She wouldn't do it otherwise."

"Do what?" Rex stormed over, looking as if he'd like to choke the agent. "Scare my aunt half to death?"

"No!" Jeremiah threw his hands up. "Motivate her. That's all we were doing. Trying to break through her writer's block."

"But it *was* scaring her," Roslyn cried. "That's why I refused to do it anymore. Even if you don't publish my book."

Jeremiah shook his head. "Well, if you hadn't bungled it, it would've worked perfectly. All the little macabre touches were supposed to stimulate Amelia."

"You mean the slashed pages and the bloody rose?" Nancy asked.

"Yes!" Jeremiah clapped his hands. "Weren't they brilliant?"

"And of course you bribed Roslyn to carry them out." Rex stooped and grabbed Jeremiah by the collar. "I think you're sick, Stone. My aunt could've been hurt in that car accident."

"But we didn't do that!" Roslyn protested. "That's what got me so worried . . . and confused. Things were happening that might've really hurt Ms. Beaufort. I got so scared, I—" She started crying again. Even Jeremiah looked concerned.

125

"Now, look here!" He shook free of Rex's grasp. "I didn't plan anything that would endanger Amelia. She's my best author!"

Nancy was puzzled now. "So the sleeping pills had nothing to do with you two?"

"What sleeping pills?" Roslyn asked, looking baffled.

Nancy quickly explained why Amelia had overslept the other morning.

"I've grown to love Amelia," Roslyn said emphatically. "I promise, Nancy, I would never hurt her."

Rex glared at Jeremiah.

"Likewise. I wanted her to write, not sleep. I thought she was getting stale and just needed a little, well, excitement to get her going again. We were going to try one more thing, but as you heard, Roslyn backed out."

"So why didn't you mail my letters?" Bess asked Roslyn.

Roslyn hung her head. "You and the rest of Amelia's fans were taking up a lot of her time. I figured you'd stop writing if you got no reply. Jeremiah told me to keep all distractions away from Amelia. I'm really sorry."

Jeremiah threw up his hands. "Listen. I'll admit I was desperate. Roslyn had confided to me that Amelia was only on Chapter One. The publishing company was breathing down my neck. And suggestions and hints weren't budging her. She just wasn't writing fast enough."

Nancy nodded. Everything Jeremiah said made sense. She knew the agent hadn't wanted to hurt Amelia, just get the publisher off his back and receive the money he was due when Amelia turned her book in.

Nancy turned to Roslyn. "Do you have any idea who else could be playing some very deadly tricks on Amelia?"

The secretary shook her head, then glanced hesitantly at Rex. "No, except . . . well, I did overhear Rex talking on the phone. And he said something about getting his aunt to sign—no matter what."

"Whoa," cried Rex as everyone looked at him. "I finally thought I'd won my gold star. If you start accusing me again, I'm out of here." He began backing toward the hall, then turned and left quickly.

"Not so fast," Bess warned.

"Let him go," Nancy said. "He was probably just talking about getting her to sell those five acres."

Jeremiah stood up, too. "I think in light of all this, I'd better pack my bags. I don't think my presence is going to help Amelia any. I'll just have to ask the publisher for more time."

"First, I think we have some explaining to do," Roslyn said. Standing up straight, she looked Jeremiah in the eye for the first time. "I want Amelia to know everything."

"You're right." The agent sighed. "Well, after

127

this, maybe I won't have a book or an author—or an agency," he muttered as they headed out the door.

"I don't know," Nancy said. "Maybe Amelia will forgive you."

The two left. Nancy and Bess watched them go. "Do you believe their story?" asked Bess, dropping down on one of the chairs in the drawing room.

Nancy shrugged. "As crazy as it sounds, it fits. They don't seem to know anything about Amelia's secret project so their actions couldn't be connected to that book." Suddenly Nancy fell silent.

"Uh-oh," Bess said. "I know that look. What are you thinking?"

"I'm wondering about that Confederate cap and Miles."

"But Louise said Miles was in the garden," Bess reminded her.

"I know," said Nancy. "But we called an hour after the driver jumped from the carriage. You said yourself the culprit was in a big hurry. Miles could've made it back here just in time."

"You're right." Bess's eyes met Nancy's. "Why would he be trying to scare Amelia?"

Nancy's eyes twinkled. "Sometimes detectives have to find evidence first, then figure out the motive."

"Oh no!" Bess groaned. "I know what you're thinking. We've got to find that Confederate uniform."

Nancy nodded. "We have the cap and the belt

buckle. We just need to find the rest of it—and with luck, the person who stole it."

Bess stood up. "Count me out. I'm not snooping around that creepy old garage or barn or whatever they call their home."

"You don't have to," Nancy assured Bess. "You just have to make sure Miles and Louise are busy somewhere else."

"Doing what?"

Nancy grinned. "Oh, you'll think of something."

"You know, I did just think of a way to do it," said Bess. She turned her back to Nancy. "Help me unclasp this locket, would you?"

Nancy undid the chain of the locket Bess wore around her neck. She handed it to her friend.

"Thanks," said Bess, dropping the locket and chain into her pocket. "Now you just sit on the back porch and wait for Miles to come into the house. Leave the rest to me."

"Okay, good luck," said Nancy, seating herself on a wicker rocking chair on the porch. She took a folded brochure she'd gotten at the museum from her pocket and pretended to read it.

She smiled when she heard Bess's voice coming from the kitchen through the open window. "I don't believe it, Louise," Bess wailed. "My chain broke just as I was bending over the sink. The locket fell into the drain."

Nancy could hear Louise's voice, but she couldn't make out her words. Bess came through loud and clear. "You mean Miles knows how to do that? He could really take a drain apart?" Bess asked innocently.

Ten minutes later Nancy saw Miles coming up the walk. He was coming from the direction of his house. Nancy assumed Louise had phoned him there. He stomped up the stairs, nodding curtly at Nancy before going into the house.

Nancy casually sauntered off the porch. When she was far enough from the house, she broke into a run to the garage. The upstairs entrance to the Brewtons' lodgings was around the back. She went up the outside stairs.

The Brewtons' three-room apartment was as spotless as the mansion's kitchen. Suddenly Nancy realized something. If anyone was in a perfect position to steal that Confederate uniform, it was Louise. The housekeeper had access to all the mansion's rooms. But why would Louise or Miles be interested in an old uniform?

Nancy glanced at the titles on the Brewtons' bookshelf. *Confederate War, The Blue and the Gray, Union Victory.* One or both of them was very interested in the Civil War. But then, a lot of southerners were, Nancy reasoned.

Nancy's eyes swept the room. There was simply no place to hide anything in this small, tidy apartment. She stepped into the kitchen. It was old-fashioned and looked as if it were hardly ever used. That made sense, Nancy figured. Louise did all her

130

cooking at the mansion. Nancy had noticed that Miles and Louise even ate in that kitchen.

A light went on in Nancy's head. She quickly began searching the kitchen. The refrigerator contained milk, butter, and a few odds and ends. The freezer was empty.

Nancy pulled open the cabinets. Pots, pans and dishes were all neatly stacked.

Then she pulled open the door to the stove oven. There, neatly folded, was a gray Confederate uniform. Nancy took it out. The first thing she checked was the belt. Sure enough, the buckle was missing. It had probably fallen off in the dark passage when Louise or Miles was taking it from the house. And there was no hat, either. Nancy felt uneasy as she noticed that one more thing was missing—the sword.

She was just about sure Miles was the driver of the carriage. Now she needed a motive.

Quickly, she let herself out of the apartment. She had almost reached the mansion when a scream ripped through the air. It came from the mansion.

Then another voice cried out. It was Amelia. "Fire!" she shrieked. "Fire!"

Nancy sprinted toward the mansion and dashed up the back porch steps. She followed the smell of the smoke down the hall—to Amelia's office.

16

Family Secrets

With a cry, Amelia started into the burning room.

Nancy grabbed her arm and pulled her back. "No!" she cried. "It's too dangerous."

"But my papers. All my work!" The woman's face was ashen as she stared at the flames.

"Where's a fire extinguisher?" asked Nancy.

Amelia waved her cane toward the hall closet. "In there."

Just then Bess came running down the stairs. When she saw the fire, she shouted for help over her shoulder.

Nancy grabbed Bess's arm. "Hold on to Amelia. Don't let her go in that room!" Then she ran for the closet.

Nancy pulled out the extinguisher just as Roslyn

came from the kitchen with one in her hand. The two of them stepped cautiously into the smoke-filled office.

They sprayed foam everywhere. Nancy concentrated on the stacks of papers. They had quickly caught fire and most of them were destroyed. Luckily, Nancy and Roslyn had been in time to keep the furniture and the rest of the house from catching fire.

Finally the last flame was smothered. Nancy lowered the extinguisher. Silently, the foursome surveyed the damage. The room was a mess.

"What happened?" Miles Brewton's voice broke the silence. Nancy turned and looked at him. For a second there was an expression of shock on his face—then he looked completely blank.

"I'll clean it up," he said gruffly.

"No!" Amelia blocked his way with her cane. "I don't want anyone touching a thing. Shut the room up. I'm going upstairs to rest. Please send up my dinner on a tray." She slowly made her way up the hall.

"You heard her," Louise said. She had been watching the scene quietly from the hall. Firmly, she closed the door on the black, soggy mess of an office. "Dinner is in an hour, Miles." Louise motioned to her husband, and the two went into the kitchen just as Jeremiah came in from outside.

"What's going on here?" he asked. Roslyn gestured toward the closed office door. "Oh my!" said the agent as he opened the door. "There goes any hope for a book in the near future."

"Don't you ever think of anyone but yourself?" Roslyn demanded.

Nancy put a hand on her arm. "Where were you both?" she asked.

Roslyn stopped cold. "You're not accusing us . . . me?"

"Yes, we are!" Bess said angrily.

"Spare me!" Jeremiah slammed the door. "This is it. I'm leaving. Amelia persuaded me to stay, though I have no idea why I listened to her. Now I have some young girl interrogating me."

"Mr. Stone." Nancy's voice was low and serious. "Some very strange things are going on around here. I need your help in finding out who's behind them. Amelia needs your help."

The agent was silent.

"We were walking in the garden," Roslyn said quietly. "I came back ahead of Jeremiah."

"Did you see Rex?" Bess asked.

"No, as a matter of fact, we didn't," said Roslyn.

Bess and Nancy looked at each other.

"I'm going upstairs to check on Amelia," Roslyn said.

"I'll go find Rex," Jeremiah volunteered. "I'm sure he'll want to know what happened."

"When you find him, tell him I'd like to talk to him," said Nancy.

After they had left, Nancy opened the office door

134

and took one last look. She noted that the window facing the back garden was open.

"Anyone could've tossed a match in here from outside," she said to Bess as she bent down to check under the window.

"Yeah," Bess agreed. "It would only have taken a second for these papers to catch on fire."

Nancy held up a tiny, charred piece of wood.

"It looks like a wooden matchstick," said Bess, "but it's hard to tell."

Nancy dropped it on the heap of burnt things. "You're right. None of our clues seem to help us move forward on this case."

Bess knelt down beside her. "Did you find anything at the Brewtons'?"

Nancy nodded. "Yep. The uniform."

"Wow! Then it *was* Miles."

"I think so," said Nancy. She stood up and surveyed the room, then looked back at Bess. "The more I think about this mystery, the more certain I am that the solution lies with Amelia and her writing. Otherwise, why would someone burn her papers? She's been keeping something from us . . . and now it's time to find out what that is."

After dinner, Bess and Nancy knocked on Amelia's bedroom door.

"Come in."

Nancy pushed the door open, and the girls peered inside. Amelia waved them in.

"I was expecting you," the woman said. She was seated in a rocker, staring out the window. "Look at that view."

The sun was setting, and the sky over the river had turned a smoky pink.

"It's beautiful," agreed Nancy.

"So you want to know why someone set my office on fire," Amelia said, still staring out the window.

"That's right," Nancy said. She sat on the floor next to Bess. "We know you've been keeping something from us," Nancy began. "We found out about the fake manuscript. We recognized it as your first book."

Amelia laughed. "Good for you, dear. Roslyn had no idea. I told her just this afternoon. Then we broke it to Jeremiah. He's not the only one who can play tricks."

"We also read your contract. You were supposed to be working on a *nonfiction* book about the Civil War," said Nancy. "Why did you keep it such a big secret—even from your agent?"

Amelia sighed. "It was to be a book about my great-grandparents. I was so excited. I thought it would be a way to learn more about my family's history as well as write an important book. I wanted to keep the project a secret because I didn't think Jeremiah, or my fans, would approve. Everyone is used to getting novels from Amelia Beaufort. Unfortunately, after I began my research, I, too, began wishing I'd stuck to fiction."

"Why? What could be so horrible that you'd want to give up the whole project?" Nancy asked.

With a sigh, Amelia picked up her cane. Using the tip of it, she pressed on the wall below the window. A small rectangle of wood popped out, revealing a hole in the wall. In the hole was a book.

Nancy reached in and pulled it out. It was bound in cracked leather and looked very old.

"My great-grandfather's journal," Amelia said. "About a year ago, when I began researching my book, I came across a letter he'd written to my great-grandmother. In it he mentioned a panel in a bedroom wall. He told her he'd hidden a gun there and that she should use it at any sign of trouble.

"Naturally, I was curious, but it took me months to find the panel. That's when I discovered the journal."

"You must have been really excited!" Bess said.

"Ecstatic. It was an answer to a writer's dreams. I was going to base my whole book on the journal."

"What happened?"

"I found out that Colonel Ashley Beaufort didn't die a hero. He died a thief and a traitor." Amelia's voice was bitter. She opened the book and carefully thumbed through to the back pages. "Why don't you read the last entry aloud." She handed it to Nancy.

Nancy cleared her throat and began to read. " 'I haven't much time. Charleston is in flames. I am preparing to dig up the gold. Lieutenant P. and I buried it at the point of the M. The lieutenant is so gullible. He thinks his family gold is going to England to be sold for arms. I even convinced him to help me bury it—I said it was the only way to safeguard it from Yankee thieves. Now I will go dig it up and add it to the fortune I've amassed by stealing from other shipments. Thank God no one will be the wiser. The ship it was intended for sank in the harbor. Now I must get it and flee with my family. There is no time.'"

When Nancy finished reading, there was a long silence.

"He stole from the Confederate army," Amelia said angrily. "It was his job to make sure the gold and jewels got on the ships to England. When he saw the South was losing, he turned on his own people."

"He must've been desperate," Bess said gently.

"I don't care!" Amelia retorted. "He is still a traitor to me and to anyone else who'd find out the truth."

"Which is why you quit writing the book?" asked Nancy.

Amelia nodded wearily. "Yes. For generations my family has prided itself on being descended from a hero. I wasn't about to reveal Ashley's disgrace to anyone, so I couldn't do the Civil War book I'd planned on surprising the world with. In the meantime Jeremiah was pressuring me, telling me my fans would desert me if there wasn't a new Amelia

Beaufort book out soon. He thought I was working on a book called 'Colonial Hero,' so I pretended my first book was that book. Since neither he nor Roslyn had ever read *Love in Atlanta,* they never caught on."

"Didn't Roslyn ever notice you working on the Civil War book?" asked Bess.

"No, my dear," Amelia replied. "Originally I'd planned on telling her about my secret project, but then I made that awful discovery about Ashley. After that, I just kept her busy typing."

As Nancy listened in silence, her mind was racing. "Amelia," she began, "if Ashley's secret was never revealed, then the gold may never have been found."

"I assume he dug it up before he died," answered Amelia. "But what became of it, I have no idea."

"What if he never got the chance to dig it up?" Nancy suggested excitedly. "What if it's still here and that's why someone has been trying to scare you?"

"I don't understand," said Amelia.

"I think somehow someone knows there's gold here," said Nancy. "And that person wants you off the estate to be free to search for it. And the only way to do that is to scare you off."

"But why is all this suddenly happening now?" Amelia asked.

"My guess is that our culprit knows you've found this journal. Before this, he or she had time. Now, whoever it is is afraid that the journal is going to give you the clue you need to find the gold first," Nancy speculated.

"Who's our main suspect now?" asked Bess.

"There's Roslyn," said Nancy. "She had access to Amelia's notes. And we know she can be bribed. She could be in it with Jeremiah. Then there are the Brewtons." Nancy placed her hand on Amelia's arm. "I found your stolen uniform at the Brewtons' apartment."

"No!" cried Amelia, shocked. "But then, Louise has always admired it. Perhaps temptation got the better of her. It doesn't prove anything. Not really."

"I have some good news, though." Nancy smiled. "I don't think Rex would try to sell off five acres of land if he thought gold might be buried on it."

"That is good news," said Amelia. "Rex hates the state of disrepair that the mansion has fallen into, but he loves the place. As a boy, he loved to play on the grounds near the rosebushes."

Suddenly Nancy's face brightened. "The rosebushes!" she cried.

"What about them?" asked Bess.

"Think. The point of the M. The rosebushes."

Amelia shook her cane excitedly. "The roses are planted in the shape of an M for Magnolia Mansion. It's not so easy to tell now, they're so straggly. But in my childhood they were pruned carefully into an M shape."

Nancy helped Amelia to her feet. "Come on,"

she said. "We've got some digging to do before it's completely dark outside."

"You and Amelia head for the roses," Nancy told Bess at the bottom of the stairs. "I'll go for a shovel."

Nancy reached the garage, glad that the windows in the Brewtons' apartment above were dark. She found a shovel and sprinted to the rose garden.

"Over here." Bess waved.

"The letter M has three points," said Amelia as Nancy joined them. "The center point, and the two points at the top. Let's start at the center point."

Nancy dug the shovel in. She dug about seven inches. Then Bess took a turn. Soon they had dug a hole about a foot deep.

Taking the shovel back from Bess, Nancy wiped her brow and began to dig again. It was dark out now, and she couldn't see much as she jabbed the shovel into the bottom of the hole in frustration. *Clunk!*

"That sounds like metal to me!" cried Bess.

Using the side of the shovel, Nancy scraped away more dirt and knelt down. Gleaming in the moonlight was the top of a box.

"I don't believe it," said Amelia in an astonished whisper.

"Step back," came a cold voice from behind Amelia. "That gold is mine."

17

Amelia's New Book

Nancy whirled around. It was Louise Brewton! She was standing behind them, a Confederate sword grasped with both hands and raised high over her head. "That gold belongs to me!" she cried.

Amelia and the girls took a few steps backward.

"Louise, please, you're going to hurt some—" Amelia began, but Louise didn't let her finish. She kicked the cane away from Amelia and with one arm grabbed her around the neck. "Wouldn't it be ironic if your great-grandfather's own traitorous blade were used against you!" she said, her eyes flashing with anger.

"That's enough, Louise!" Miles Brewton called, running toward them. "I said, enough."

"Go away, Miles," Louise snapped. "This doesn't concern you."

"Yes, it does," he protested. "I've had enough of your obsession."

"What am I supposed to do, Miles?" Louise ranted, still holding Amelia tight. "Should I forget that Ashley Beaufort stole my family's fortune? Should I forget that the high and mighty Beauforts have been parading around like saints when they're really descended from a thief and a traitor? Should I forget that members of the Pringle family now work as servants because Ashley Beaufort stole all their money?"

"Your great-grandfather was Lieutenant P. in the journal, wasn't he?" Nancy said.

"He certainly was," Louise replied. "He discovered that Ashley Beaufort had swindled him, but it was too late. Charleston was burning and he died defending it. But my great-grandmother lived, and she knew of Beaufort's guilt, even though no one believed her."

"That was long ago—" Amelia started to say.

"Family honor is family honor," Louise snarled. Slowly, she lowered the sword to Amelia's throat.

Nancy sprang forward, hurling herself at Louise. Louise staggered back, letting go of Amelia and dropping the sword. Nancy grabbed the housekeeper by the waist and pulled her to the ground.

Immediately, Bess was beside Nancy. She pinned Louise's arms to the ground.

Rex rushed up, an open shirt flung over his pajamas. "I saw some of what was happening from the window," he said. "I called the police."

"Good," said Nancy, getting up off Louise. Bess let go, too, and Miles helped his wife to her feet.

"Louise's family has been obsessed for years with finding the gold," Miles explained. His voice sounded flat and weary. "But no one in the family knew where it was buried."

"Is that why the two of you worked on the estate for all these years?" asked Amelia, leaning heavily on Rex.

Miles nodded. "She convinced me we would find the gold someday, and then we'd just quietly leave. Everything would have been fine if you hadn't started researching that book. Louise saw some of your notes about the Civil War project while she was cleaning. She was convinced that you were on the trail of the gold. And once you found the journal, we got desperate."

"But how did she know I'd found it?" asked Amelia.

"Because you talk in your sleep," Louise snarled. "You were asleep in a chair one day. You started ranting about the awful truth in the book. You mumbled about stolen gold."

"You do talk in your sleep," said Bess gently. "I've heard you myself."

144

"So you were desperate enough to cut my aunt's brakes? And drop a chandelier on her head?" said Rex angrily. "You didn't even care if you hurt innocent guests, too?"

Miles nodded, looking at the ground. "We've spent our whole lives looking for that gold," he said quietly. "The thought of losing it was too much."

The sound of police sirens filled the air. At the same time, Jeremiah and Roslyn ran toward them from the house. In the confusion, Louise jerked from her husband's grasp.

She threw herself on the hole Nancy and Bess had dug and began clawing the dirt. "I've found it!" she sobbed. "After all these years I've found the gold!"

"So what's going to happen to Louise and Miles?" Roslyn asked the next morning at breakfast.

"We're pressing charges, of course," Rex answered. "They could've seriously hurt someone."

He pushed back his chair, having already wolfed down his eggs and bacon. Nancy and Bess had fixed a farewell breakfast for everyone.

"I'm hoping Louise will receive some help," Amelia told them. "Her obsession took over her life." She shook her head. "To think that all these years I thought the Brewtons were family."

"With family like that, you wouldn't need enemies," Bess said. "I mean, they were the perfect team. Louise, the housekeeper, always knew who was going where and doing what."

"Then she had Miles do the dirty work," Nancy added. "Like pretending to be the carriage driver. And sabotaging the boat."

"You wonder how Louise convinced Miles to go along with her," Roslyn said.

"Greed and love, dear child, are the oldest motivators in the world," Jeremiah chimed in, setting down his coffee cup.

"But why did they attack you girls?" asked Roslyn.

"Louise must have eavesdropped either on my first phone conversation with Amelia or from the secret passageway," Nancy explained. "She found out right away we were here to help Amelia and figured sooner or later one of us would get to the bottom of what was happening at the mansion. She wanted to scare us off the case."

Bess shuddered. "It nearly worked the day the chandelier almost hit us. I was ready to go home."

Jeremiah cleared his throat. "I guess Roslyn and I didn't help matters any. Our dramatic touches to get Amelia writing fitted right in with their scheme."

Nancy nodded. "Both you and Rex helped keep the focus off them by being perfect suspects."

Rex chuckled. "Thank goodness that's over."

"I agree," said Jeremiah. "Now Amelia can get to

146

work on her new book. I think we'll have a best-seller on our hands."

"It's called *Charleston Bride*," Amelia told them. "It's all about my great-grandmother and her children's hospital. I'll add the part about my great-grandfather's smuggling to spice it up."

"You don't care if it tarnishes your family's history?" asked Bess.

"I've learned one thing from all this," said Amelia. "The past is the past. I don't want to end up obsessed with it like poor Louise. Besides, I've donated the coins to the historical society. That should insure my standing in Charleston society."

"Aunt Amelia, you didn't!" cried Rex.

"Don't worry, dear boy." Amelia laughed. "I kept enough aside to spruce this place up and pay the bills—without the sale of five acres."

Rex smiled broadly. "That's the first good news I've heard in a long time."

Jeremiah raised his glass of orange juice. "Let's drink a toast to Amelia's new book."

They clinked glasses. "To be dedicated to Nancy Drew and Bess Marvin," Amelia added.

When they'd finished their juice, Rex stood up. "Are you two packed for the airport?" he asked Nancy and Bess.

"Yes. But that reminds me," said Bess. "I can't find my new lipstick. It was in my makeup case."

Nancy grinned mischievously. "I believe I saw

147

Rex rummaging through your case just the other day. Maybe he has it."

Rex groaned loudly. "I can't win with you two. Don't you ever give up?"

Nancy shook her head, then grinned widely. "Never."

NANCY DREW® MYSTERY STORIES By Carolyn Keene

- ☐ THE TRIPLE HOAX—#57
  69153-8 $3.50
- ☐ THE FLYING SAUCER MYSTERY—#58
  72320-0 $3.50
- ☐ THE SECRET IN THE OLD LACE—#59
  69067-1 $3.99
- ☐ THE GREEK SYMBOL MYSTERY—#60
  67457-9 $3.50
- ☐ THE SWAMI'S RING—#61
  62467-9 $3.50
- ☐ THE KACHINA DOLL MYSTERY—#62
  67220-7 $3.50
- ☐ THE TWIN DILEMMA—#63
  67301-7 $3.99
- ☐ CAPTIVE WITNESS—#64
  70471-0 $3.50
- ☐ MYSTERY OF THE WINGED LION—#65
  62681-7 $3.50
- ☐ RACE AGAINST TIME—#66
  69485-5 $3.50
- ☐ THE SINISTER OMEN—#67
  73938-7 $3.50
- ☐ THE ELUSIVE HEIRESS—#68
  62478-4 $3.99
- ☐ CLUE IN THE ANCIENT DISGUISE—#69
  64279-0 $3.50
- ☐ THE BROKEN ANCHOR—#70
  74228-0 $3.50
- ☐ THE SILVER COBWEB—#71
  70992-5 $3.50
- ☐ THE HAUNTED CAROUSEL—#72
  66227-9 $3.50
- ☐ ENEMY MATCH—#73
  64283-9 $3.50
- ☐ MYSTERIOUS IMAGE—#74
  69401-4 $3.50
- ☐ THE EMERALD-EYED CAT MYSTERY—#75
  64282-0 $3.50
- ☐ THE ESKIMO'S SECRET—#76
  73003-7 $3.50
- ☐ THE BLUEBEARD ROOM—#77
  66857-9 $3.50
- ☐ THE PHANTOM OF VENICE—#78
  73422-9 $3.50
- ☐ THE DOUBLE HORROR
  OF FENLEY PLACE—#79
  64387-8 $3.50
- ☐ THE CASE OF THE DISAPPEARING
  DIAMONDS—#80
  64896-9 $3.50
- ☐ MARDI GRAS MYSTERY—#81
  64961-2 $3.50

- ☐ THE CLUE IN THE CAMERA—#82
  64962-0 $3.50
- ☐ THE CASE OF THE VANISHING VEIL—#83
  63413-5 $3.50
- ☐ THE JOKER'S REVENGE—#84
  63414-3 $3.50
- ☐ THE SECRET OF SHADY GLEN—#85
  63416-X $3.50
- ☐ THE MYSTERY OF MISTY CANYON—#86
  63417-8 $3.99
- ☐ THE CASE OF THE RISING STARS—#87
  66312-7 $3.50
- ☐ THE SEARCH FOR CINDY AUSTIN—#88
  66313-5 $3.50
- ☐ THE CASE OF THE DISAPPEARING DEEJAY—#89
  66314-3 $3.50
- ☐ THE PUZZLE AT PINEVIEW SCHOOL—#90
  66315-1 $3.95
- ☐ THE GIRL WHO COULDN'T REMEMBER—#91
  66316-X $3.50
- ☐ THE GHOST OF CRAVEN COVE—#92
  66317-8 $3.50
- ☐ THE CASE OF THE SAFECRACKER'S SECRET—#93
  66318-6 $3.50
- ☐ THE PICTURE PERFECT MYSTERY—#94
  66315-1 $3.50
- ☐ THE SILENT SUSPECT—#95
  69280-1 $3.50
- ☐ THE CASE OF THE PHOTO FINISH—#96
  69281-X $3.99
- ☐ THE MYSTERY AT MAGNOLIA MANSION—#97
  69282-8 $3.99
- ☐ THE HAUNTING OF HORSE ISLAND—#98
  69284-4 $3.50
- ☐ THE SECRET AT SEVEN ROCKS—#99
  69285-2 $3.50
- ☐ A SECRET IN TIME—#100
  69286-0 $3.50
- ☐ THE MYSTERY OF THE MISSING MILLIONAIRESS—#101
  69287-9 $3.50
- ☐ THE SECRET IN THE DARK—#102
  69279-8 $3.50
- ☐ THE STRANGER IN THE SHADOWS—#103
  73049-5 $3.50
- ☐ THE MYSTERY OF THE JADE TIGER—#104
  73050-9 $3.50
- ☐ THE CLUE IN THE ANTIQUE TRUNK—#105
  73051-7 $3.99
- ☐ THE CASE OF THE ARTFUL CRIME—#106
  73052-5 $3.99
- ☐ NANCY DREW® GHOST STORIES—#1
  69132-5 $3.50

and don't forget...THE HARDY BOYS® Now available in paperback

Simon & Schuster, Mail Order Dept. ND5
200 Old Tappan Road, Old Tappan, NJ 07675
Please send me copies of the books checked. Please add appropriate local sales tax.
☐ Enclosed full amount per copy with this coupon (Send check or money order only.)
Please be sure to include proper postage and handling:
95¢—first copy
50¢—each additonal copy ordered.

☐ If order is for $10.00 or more, you may charge to one of the following accounts:
☐ Mastercard   ☐ Visa

Name _____   Credit Card No. _____

Address _____

City _____   Card Expiration Date _____

State _____ Zip _____   Signature _____

Books listed are also available at your local bookstore. Prices are subject to change without notice.   NDD-45

THE HARDY BOYS® SERIES By Franklin W. Dixon

When Your Teacher Is From
OUTERSPACE
School is Anything but Boring!

Bestselling author **Bruce Coville** brings you adventure and excitement in these thrilling books.

My Teacher is an Alien

Susan and Peter's class has been invaded and it's up to them to save the sixth grade from a fate worse than math tests!

My Teacher Fried My Brains

The seventh grade is sizzling and Duncan must figure out which of the new teachers is the alien—before his brains, and the planet, are fried to a pulp!

My Teacher Glows in the Dark

Peter is off on the field trip of a lifetime—to outerspace with a spaceship full of aliens!

Watch for *My Teacher Flunked the Planet* in June 1992